THE
FORGOTTEN
KING

THE FORGOTTEN KING

Edward the Elder

LAURIE PAGE

The Book Guild Ltd

First published in Great Britain in 2022 by
The Book Guild Ltd
Unit E2 Airfield Business Park,
Harrison Road, Market Harborough,
Leicestershire. LE16 7UL
Tel: 0116 2792299
www.bookguild.co.uk
Email: info@bookguild.co.uk
Twitter: @bookguild

Copyright © 2022 Laurie Page

The right of Laurie Page to be identified as the author of this
work has been asserted by them in accordance with the
Copyright, Design and Patents Act 1988.

All rights reserved. No part of this publication may be
reproduced, transmitted, or stored in a retrieval system, in any form or by any means,
without permission in writing from the publisher, nor be otherwise circulated in
any form of binding or cover other than that in which it is published and without
a similar condition being imposed on the subsequent purchaser.

This work is entirely fictitious and bears no resemblance to any persons living or dead.

Typeset in 11pt Minion Pro

Printed and bound by CPI Group (UK) Ltd, Croydon, CR0 4YY

ISBN 978 1915122 285

British Library Cataloguing in Publication Data.
A catalogue record for this book is available from the British Library.

In memory of my father: Frank Richard Page

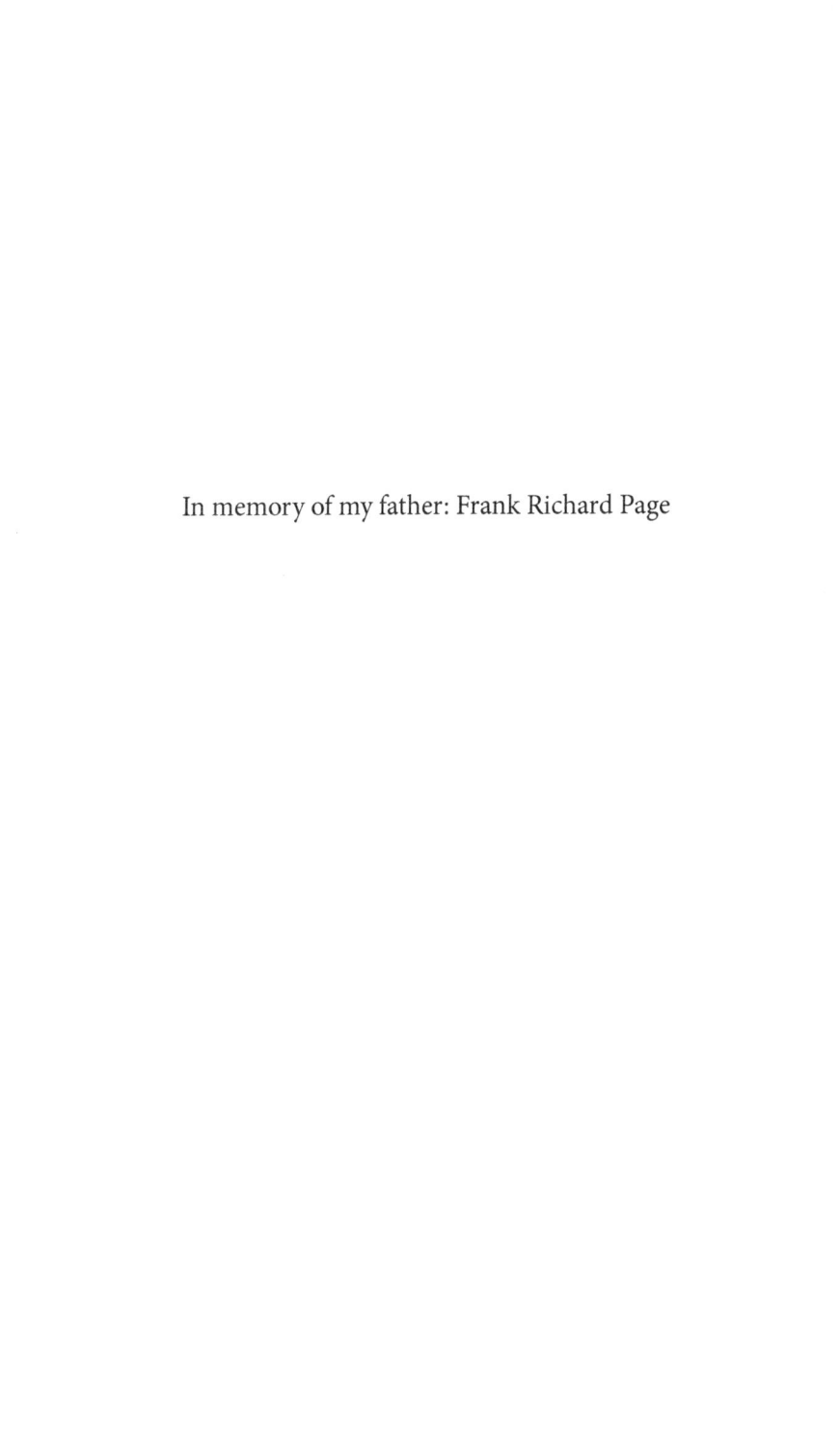

CONTENTS

Acknowledgements		ix
Introduction		xi
Chapter 1	The History Class	1
Chapter 2	The Year 899	3
Chapter 3	The Year 902	19
Chapter 4	The Year 906	39
Chapter 5	The Year 908	47
Chapter 6	The Year 910	66
Chapter 7	The Year 912	76
Chapter 8	The Year 914	85
Chapter 9	The Year 916	107
Chapter 10	The Year 917	111
Chapter 11	The Year 918	128
Chapter 12	The Year 920	141
Chapter 13	The Year 924	153
Chapter 14	The Find	162

Appendix 1	The Saxon Family Trees	171
Appendix 2	Historical and Fictional Characters	172
Appendix 3	The Saxon Burghs 910 to 921	177
Appendix 4	Edward's Children	179
Appendix 5	Timeline	181

References and Further Reading	183
About the Author	187
Index	189

ACKNOWLEDGEMENTS

I would like to thank my friend Rob Lee, an avid reader of historical novels, for reading through the first draft and suggesting some useful amendments.

Also, Ellora Bennett for reading through the manuscript and providing a professional view regarding the historical accuracy of the novel. Ellora has a BA (1st) in History and the Medieval World (University of Winchester). She won the King Alfred Prize for Best Performance in History in 2014. She gained a MA in History (University of Winchester). She is currently at the Freie Universistat, Berlin, studying a DPhil in pre-Viking warfare in England.

INTRODUCTION

This is a story set in Anglo-Saxon England. But a story set around known events between 899 and 924 when Edward the Elder reigned as King of Wessex and the Saxon people. Not that the historical events during the tenth century provide much detail. Apart from the *Anglo-Saxon Chronicles*, of which there was more than one version due to the location of their authorship, and very few other sources, some of which were written a number of years later, there is little documentary evidence to tell us of the life and times of early tenth-century Anglo-Saxon England. We know very little of the personality or even a description of the most prominent people of the day. Although the *Chronicles* might tell of a battle victory and the names of the leaders who fought and died, there is no knowing the number of men on each side or a detailed strategy or account of how the battle unfolded.

I have used various terms for the invading Vikings: Danes, Pagans, Heathens, Norwegians and Norsemen are all synonymous as the sources themselves often used the terms interchangeably. The Saxons, who by this time seem to have predominantly become Christian, would have regarded these invaders as un-Christian, hence the terms Pagans and Heathens. Likewise, the 'Saxon' migrants in the fifth century had originally included Angles (East Anglia) and Jutes (Kent), but I have used the term Saxon to represent what had become the English people.

Maldon existed probably as a Saxon community by this time, although there is no knowing the size of such a community in the early tenth century. This has been estimated by the numbers supplied in the Domesday Book of 1086 sometime later. So I have used this as a fictional location for this story about the members of a family that governed there. This community has been portrayed as loyal to the King because there is no mention of any opposition to his visit in 912 and it seems unlikely that he would visit three time in six years if he felt he was not welcome there.

I have corrupted the spelling of many of the Saxon characters to make interpretation of the names easier. The Saxons did not have surnames as such. Their Christian names were often made up of two elements and usually the first part used to indicate descent so that King Athelwolf (Alfred's father) had sons Aethelbert and Aethelwold, and Edward had a son, Edwin. Where the names are spelled with *ae*, such as *Aethelwold*, this would probably have been with the pronunciation like *say* (as opposed to *sat*). I have sometimes dropped the *a* or *e* for easier pronunciation.

Where the location of the events has been stated, if possible I have also indicated what that place would have been known by the Saxons or Old English.

CHAPTER 1
THE HISTORY CLASS
A SECONDARY SCHOOL IN ESSEX

'So what you are saying then, Sir, is that Edward I should not really have been Edward I but Edward IV?'

'That's exactly what I'm saying, Leo.' Mr Burchell strolled across the classroom. 'The first King of all England was considered to be Athelstan, but his father Edward the Elder was virtually King of England by the end of his reign. He was called "The Elder" because after him, another Edward, the Martyr, had briefly been King and Edward the Confessor, the last Saxon King before King Harold, had reigned for many years. So the Edward who came to the throne a long time after, in 1239, was the fourth Edward.'

Leo fidgeted awkwardly in his chair. 'So how come the previous Edwards weren't recognised?'

'Good question! Possibly the Normans discredited their Saxon rivals, just as the Tudors had had tried to destroy the reputation of Richard III and their House of York predecessors. Yet Edward the Confessor ruled for twenty-four years from 1042 until his death in 1066 and was revered by later kings as a saint. Edward the Elder was a great military leader and, together with his son Athelstan, managed to defeat the invading Danes in some major battles and take control of most of the area we now call England.'

'I haven't even heard of Edward the Elder.' Many of the class of 3B were thinking exactly the same thing.

'Well, that's nothing to feel embarrassed about, Leo. Few people have. Edward is a forgotten King of England and deserves much more credit than he has received. Let me tell you about him.'

CHAPTER 2
THE YEAR 899
WINCHESTER (WINTANCAESTER)

King Alfred lay dying in his chamber at Winchester Palace. The sun was sinking as if to reflect Alfred's life, and as darkness descended, candles were lit in abundance all around the King. It was October and a good fire glowed within the hall. Alfred's wife, Ealswith, was perched on the side of the bed. The King's daughter Athelflaed, who had made a special trip from her home in Mercia, his youngest son Athelweard, Edward's wife Ecgwynn, Archbishop Plegmund and three ealdormen who were the important men of the land were present and all gathered around the King's bed.

Alfred had mumbled that he should like to speak with Edward, his eldest son, and enquired of his whereabouts. But Edward had not yet arrived. After hearing the news of his father he was travelling in haste from Hertford, riding ahead of his military force, which had been engaged in skirmishes with the Danes.

He knew it was important to be present if his father died, as the Witan, the King's Council, had to approve the new king, and Edward knew that there was another contender to the throne, so he was not taking it for granted that he would succeed without opposition.

As he rode towards Winchester with his small band of loyal followers in the dusky light he felt relieved that he would reach the city before nightfall. But he also felt great sorrow for his father, whom he had fought beside, laughed and cried with, and often talked and argued with into the late hours of the night. He also knew that he would have to inherit the perpetual conflict with the marauding Danes that his father's kingdom had been locked in, and if he succeeded as king he would need immense strength and fortitude as leader of the Saxons.

At last he burst into the King's room. Edward was twenty-five years of age, tall, with broad shoulders, and slim but muscular. He had a long face with a dark, neatly trimmed beard, and many said that he closely resembled his father in looks. He briefly greeted his wife, from whom he had been away for several weeks.

'Does he live?'

The archbishop looked despondent. 'He barely breathes, Sire.'

Edward would have liked to have been able to talk one last time with the King, but his sister explained that the King was no longer conscious, so a last conversation with his father seemed very unlikely. The eminent bystanders all watched and waited whilst the physicians tried in vain to keep Alfred alive. A few hours later, in the early hours of the morning, Alfred let out a long gasp as he quietly slipped away.

Edward immediately sent out messengers to spread the news of the King's death to the absent members of the Witan and requested that they immediately come to Winchester. Then he ordered the gates of the royal residence to be locked. It was important to Edward that he be recognised as King and elected as soon as possible. The Saxon Kingdom of Wessex needed stability in this time of crisis.

Two days later, the members of the Witan who had been able to reach Winchester gathered in the Great Hall. There were several West Saxon ealdormen, the archbishop and the bishops. They arranged for the following week, the details of burial in The Minster, the old cathedral in Winchester. More important still, they had to decide the future of the kingdom and who would be King of Wessex and the people who lived in that kingdom. The Witan consisted of the archbishops and many bishops, the military leaders who had served Alfred so steadfastly, and many old and trusted ealdormen who had been councillors and advisors to Alfred. They sat around the large, long table in the Great Hall.

Plegmund was about to open the proceedings when the muttering of the men about him suddenly ceased and he followed their gaze to the doorway. There stood a thin, elderly man with a long beard wearing a monk's habit. He approached the table. 'Asser, welcome!' The much revered and respected Welsh monk, who was now Bishop of Sherborne, had been very close to Alfred, and he was still engaged in writing the King's biography. He joined all the men at the table.

'Thank you. I have had a long journey and I am feeling rather tired. Is there any refreshment?'

Plegmund signalled to one of the servants by the door, who hurried off to find some bread and cheese and ale for the wise old man.

'So,' Plegmund began, 'we have here the will of our beloved and departed King Alfred. He designates his son Edward as his rightful heir. Of course this view may be biased, but Edward has been trained in the art of kingship and has proved himself in battle with the Pagans. He is bold, brave and, I believe, level-headed.'

'There is only one other legitimate contender,' announced Asser.

'Yes, but Aethelwold has made no representation and has had little involvement in the business of running the kingdom.'

'True.' Asser turned to one of the younger ealdormen, whose look revealed his curiosity, and felt the need to explain the past history. 'When Alfred became king his older brother Ethelred, who had been king before him, had two young sons, but they were not yet old enough to rule and the Witan therefore supported Alfred as Ethelred's successor. 'Now that King Alfred is dead, he naturally wanted his own son to succeed him, but Aethelwold, Ethelred's surviving youngest son, also has a claim to the Kingdom of Wessex. He was virtually ignored in King Alfred's will, left with just a few estates in Surrey and little more.'

'I believe that Edward would make a worthy king and invite all here to give their support.' Plegmund looked up for the approval of the gathering. Asser nodded and within the hour the Witan had voted and unanimously pledged their support for Edward as King of Wessex and the Saxon nation.

'May I suggest that the coronation take place next June on the boundary of our great kingdoms of Mercia and Wessex at Kingston on the banks of the River Thames?' announced the archbishop, himself a Mercian. 'This is where Edward's great-grandfather King Egbert held his Great Council.'

'After you crown him king, a feast day should follow to celebrate the new regime,' added Asser.

Denewulf, the learned Bishop of Winchester, spoke up. 'Yes, we can meet before Yule to discuss the coronation. We need to draw up a guest list, formulate the arrangements for the ceremony, and prepare the food and inventory for the banquet that follows.'

'The ceremonial sword of King Alfred should also be presented at the ceremony.'

Alfred's sword was a beautifully crafted blade with a bejewelled hilt highlighted by a large red garnet in the centre.

For another hour the Witan discussed further Edward's character, his assets and his weaknesses, and also the rivals and enemies he may face. The situation of the Viking threat was also considered. At the end they requested Edward be summoned to appear before them and he duly appeared minutes later to hear their verdict.

But even as the Witan sat around the table, before they could disperse, a horse messenger arrived at Winchester and provided Denewulf with crucial information. The bishop entered into the Great Hall, where he bowed to Edward and delivered his report that Danish longboats had landed on the Northumbrian coast, and, worse, Edward also learnt that his Saxon cousin and rival, Aethelwold, was making his claim to the throne.

'So what news of Aethelwold now?' Edward demanded.

Denewulf stepped forward. 'Sire, our information is that he has gathered a force and has marched on the royal site of Wimborne Minster, where his father, King Ethelred, was buried. We have been told that he has taken the town and seized a nun from the convent there.'

Aethelwold was less than forty miles from Winchester. Edward decisively began preparations in his mind for an assault on the town of Wimborne. But before he could assemble his army, the burial of his father was an important ceremony that had to take place first.

The next day, the townsfolk lined the short route from the palace to the minster to pay their respects. The great King's body was pulled on a wagon by four black horses to the minster, followed by his family and all the-important magnates, bishops and ealdormen that had come to Winchester. He was carried into the cathedral by his most loyal warriors, the thegns that were his personal bodyguard, and afterwards the archbishop performed the burial ceremony. Then the great King was laid to rest beneath the altar.

But as Edward watched the events before him, he was already considering a new minster to be built alongside the old one. He would summon the archbishop and call on the architects and master builders with the best reputation in the land to build an abbey, which would be a fitting memorial to his father and a place where the people of Winchester would be proud to worship.

There was no more time to lose. Within days Edward called on his men to equip themselves for the two-day march towards Wimborne. His men prepared their weapons, sharpening their swords and spears, and repairing their round shields. By this time they learnt that Aethelwold had also taken the manor of Christchurch, known as Twinham, the neighbour to the south of Wimborne.

Edward said goodbye to his wife and children; his eldest son Athelstan, who was only five years old, pleaded with his father to let him go with him, but Edward laughed. 'You are too young, little one, but your time will come,' he declared.

Edward's wife Egwina found it hard to raise a smile. It was difficult being married to a Saxon warrior King; the nature of the times was that in the tenth century, England was engaged in constant war with the Vikings and battles were a part of life. But there was another reason why she looked so forlorn; her son Athelstan was to be sent north to the kingdom of Mercia to be raised as a future king by Edward's sister Athelflaed and her husband Ethelred, the Lord of Mercia. This had been the wish of King Alfred and would bind the Kingdoms of Wessex and Mercia closer together. Moreover, with Edward away fighting as leader and King of the Saxons, Athelstan would one day need the protection of his Uncle Ethelred and Aunt Athelflaed, two people Edward could trust. Egwina had persuaded her husband, however, that the time was not yet right. 'Let me hang on to him until he is seven,' she pleaded.

When it was time to go it was a tearful goodbye for both Athelstan and his mother. 'You must be brave,' said Edward to his son, 'for you will be king and a great man someday.' But little Athelstan looked confused and didn't like the idea of not seeing his father. He started to cry.

As the Mercians rode back to Gloucester with Ethelred and Athelflaed, Edward bade them farewell and took his army westwards to Wimborne. They wound their way through the Wessex countryside along old tracks established by the old Britons and some Roman roads, through heathland, fields and woodland. After two days' march, as the light was fading on the second day, Edward reached an old hill fort called Bradbury Rings, constructed by the ancient Britons hundreds of years before. Edward looked around him. 'This is where we will set up camp. If Aethelwold has his scouts around, it will offer excellent protection for us overnight. We will rise at dawn tomorrow morning. Make sure our army is in readiness for a short march to Wimborne when we attack the town at the earliest opportunity.' The men pitched their tents and lit their torches. A heavy watch was stationed on the hill fort entrances throughout the night.

The next day Edward hastily dressed and roused his men. But there was a surprise waiting for Edward and his army. As he approached Wimborne he could see that the gates to the town were open and there was a welcoming party standing at the entrance. He took a party of his best men and cautiously rode towards the town gates.

The reeve and leader of the town stepped forward nervously. 'W-welcome to Wimborne, Lord.' He was sweating and shaking.

He knew that harbouring Aethelwold would not go down well with Edward, who snapped a reply. 'Where is Aethelwold? Why does he not face me in battle?'

'He has fled, Lord.'

'Where?'

'I… I know not. But I overheard his conversation with his companion. I think he has journeyed north to negotiate with the Danes.'

Edward nodded and gave a sarcastic grin. 'Yes, I can well believe this. And you, Reeve…?'

'I am loyal to you, My Lord, I had no choice – he arrived with armed men. I—'

'You are no longer commander here. You will be subordinate to my brother Aethelweard.'

The Wimborne man breathed a sigh of relief. Men had been put to the sword for less.

Edward turned to his younger brother beside him. 'Aethelweard, you are leader here. Take control of the town and organise its defences. Keep me informed of any news of Aethelwold. We will eat and rest a while and then to Christchurch to reclaim that town before we return to Winchester.'

Although only nineteen, the King had faith in his very able young brother, who would return to Winchester once the town defences were secure. Edward then summoned one of his young thegns and best warriors. 'Take a hundred men, Edmund, and make haste on the main road north through Salisbury and see if you can catch up with Aethelwold. I wager that he has a very small band of men with him, as speed will be of the essence for him.' Edward knew that Edmund was loyal to him, as he had been to his father before him. But the chance of capturing his foe was remote. The thegn, who was a giant of a man and intimidating to his enemies, nodded and mounted his horse. He was used to fighting but hoped that he had the strength to carry out his task.

Edward contemplated the situation. He knew now that Aethelwold was his rival and enemy who wanted nothing less than to be King of the Saxons, and that this would not end until one of them had been defeated and killed or captured in battle. He ordered to strike camp so that they could make their way to Christchurch and secure the town.

Edward sat with his head in his hands. He rose from his chair and began to pace the room, feeling agitated. The physician had advised the King to stay out of the bedchamber, where his wife Ecgwynn was about to give birth. But that was hours ago and the screams of pain and anguish that had let rip from behind the bedroom door had now subsided. The ominous quiet that had descended seemed to signify that their problems were far from over. Edward glanced at Athelweard, who could see his brother's frustration. 'The midwife and the physician will do their best, Edward.'

But when the physician appeared a few moments later, the look on his face was enough to disclose to Athelweard that his brother was about to hear very bad news.

'Oh no. Please, God, not Ecgwynn.' Edward rushed into the bedchamber and knelt by the bed, grabbing the blood-covered sheet as he stared in disbelief at the lifeless body before him.

'I... I am very sorry, Sire,' the physician stammered. 'There was nothing I could do. I was called too late. The baby is alive but appears to have breathing difficulties.'

Athelweard placed his hand on Edward's shoulder. He knew that there had been complications and that death during childbirth was common. It was a risk for both mother and baby. Hardly any consolation in the present situation. He tried to think rationally about who should be informed and how he would break the news to little Athelstan, who had been quite excited about the prospect of having a baby brother.

Two days later the tiny baby boy who had entered the world amid so much trauma left it without a fight. He was buried alongside his mother.

As Yule approached Edward gazed gloomily out of the window at the grey December day. He had not really recovered from the death of his wife six weeks previously and was feeling downhearted. Moreover, Athelwold was still at large and although his coronation was to take place the next April, it troubled him to think that after being crowned there may remain some support for his rival, especially from the Danes.

Asser and Archbishop Plegmund were discussing matters of state and drawing up charters. They were meeting with a number of ealdormen, who were disputing land and territory, trying to adjudicate matters. For extensive lands they required Edward's approval. They needed his input over one such case, although they were rather tentative about conversing with him as the King had been rather grumpy recently and although usually affable, had a reputation for his rare but occasional bad temper.

Asser, though, had many years' experience of dealing with Alfred, who had a similar temperament, and he approached the King armed with a parchment of importance. 'My Lord, do you recall the death of Ealdorman

THE FORGOTTEN KING

SHOWING THE SAXON KINGDOMS

Athelhelm of Wiltshire a few years ago?'

Edward tried to focus. 'Oh yes, we did not settle his land, if I remember. It was because he had no son and heir to succeed him.'

'You have a good memory, Sire. There were substantial areas of land amounting to many hides in Chippenham, Malmesbury and as far south as Salisbury.'

'So where this is taking us, Asser?'

'Well, although Athelhelm had no son, as you rightly say, he did have a daughter, Aelfflaed, who at the time was too young to inherit.'

'Yes, I remember her, I think. Pretty red-haired girl with freckles whose mother was an Irish noblewoman.'

Asser smiled and glanced over at Denewulf, who was grinning broadly.

'What are you two grinning at?'

'More than pretty,' said Denewulf quietly.

'Oh?'

'The point is, Lord, that she has now come of age and is claiming title to the land.'

Denewulf fidgeted. 'If you would like to meet with her, she is waiting in the ante-room, Sire.'

'Yes, show her in.'

The two bishops left and Denewulf returned with Aelfflaed, who stood before the King and curtseyed.

Edward looked up and just for a few seconds was dumbstruck by the beautiful woman before him. Long hair curled around her shoulders with a hint of auburn colour and she had a very pretty oval-shaped face with perfectly unblemished skin. She was of medium height with a voluptuous figure.

'Thank you, Denewulf, you may leave us. Please let us not be disturbed.' Denewulf bowed and left the room.

'Welcome, lady. Come and sit beside me.'

'Oh. Thank you, My Lord.'

'And how old are you? It must have been about four years ago when I saw you last.'

'I am twenty, My Lord, but in three weeks' time I will be twenty-one.'

'So you wish to inherit your father's land?'

'If that is acceptable. My father's will left everything to my brother but they were both killed together, fighting for King Alfred.'

'Sorry to hear that. Your father was always loyal to the King. And you have no other siblings?'

Aelfflaed shook her head.

'And how will you protect your property?'

'Well, I have a good thegn and I can hire more men to protect me.'

'But you have extensive lands. If you inherit everything you will be one of the richest landowners in England.'

'Perhaps I will marry a rich ealdorman. Maybe a nobleman!'

'Or even a king!' Edward smiled.

Aelfflaed blushed slightly. She was not sure what he meant, but she looked intently at Edward. He was now aged twenty-five, tall, broad and handsome, with a very warm smile when he chose to use it.

'Anyway, if I was attacked by Danish warriors I would hope that as I am not far away, my King would come and help a maiden in distress!'

Edward laughed. 'Why don't you come to court here at

Winchester? I can provide a house nearby for you.'

She pondered for a moment. 'May I have time to consider that, My Lord?'

'You can call me Edward. And I will grant you your lands.'

'Thank you, My Lord… um, Edward.' She beamed.

'You can kiss your King,' and Edward offered his cheek to Aelfflaed, but as she leant over towards him just at the last moment he turned his head and kissed her full on the lips. She gasped in surprise, but Edward could see she had a smirk on her face.

The King's eyes sparkled. 'Before you leave, would you like me to show you around Winchester?'

'Ooh, yes, please, I was just a little girl when I was here last with my father.'

Edward took her by the hand and showed her around the royal palace. Then they both wrapped up in warm cloaks and he took her to see the treasury with the King's jewellery and the armoury. Then, with Denewulf's permission, they briefly visited the bishop's house and the minster, and afterwards wandered through the streets of Winchester followed closely by Edmund, the King's thegn and bodyguard. They saw the Royal Mint, one of the watermills in the city and a new row of houses being built. The King explained that Aelfflaed could occupy the end house if that was her wish. They returned to the palace for some refreshment and sat once more in the Great Hall.

'I will get Bishop Denewulf to put in writing the land settlement giving you ownership.'

'Thank you, Edward, and thank you for the tour of the town.'

Edward came close to Aelfflaed and stood before her.

'It has been a very enjoyable afternoon.' He kissed her on the cheek. She suddenly threw her arms around the King's neck, thinking how audacious she was being, but she knew that the King had taken a shine to her and decided to throw caution to the wind. Edward smiled and held her close. She kissed him, a long, lingering kiss.

'So what are your plans?'

'Well, I suppose I will return to Salisbury and make arrangements to secure my land. I need to find a husband who will help me run the estate and look after me. My wish is to have many children.'

'I would like more children too. A king has to have more than one son to ensure a smooth succession after he is gone. If anything were to happen to Athelstan, God forbid, then with no successor, England could descend into chaos. No, actually, I meant what are your plans for today. Do you have to leave?'

'Oh, well, um, not really, there is no rush for me to return.'

Edward took her hand and for a while they gazed into each other's eyes. Then Edward took her by the hand and led the wide-eyed Aelfflaed into the bedchamber.

They were married the following spring by Denewulf in the minster, three weeks before the King's coronation. Aelfflaed got her wish; in the coming years she was to provide Edward with no less than eight children!

CHAPTER 3
THE YEAR 902
MALDON (MAELDUN)

Edwin brushed his fair hair away from his eyes and climbed up the hill overlooking the River Blackwater. It was a beautiful, sunny spring morning, with cotton wool-like clouds drifting slowly above him. He was feeling quite pleased with himself, having managed to bag a rabbit with an arrow from his bow, the dead animal slung over his shoulder.

Not too far distant was the Saxon community where he was heading. From its humble beginnings of just a few families, Maldon was fast becoming a good-sized community, now with over thirty houses. Outside the ditch and wooden fence that enclosed the Saxon cob houses, sheep grazed and his older brother Cuthbert was helping round up the cattle. Edwin's father Aldwine, the elder and the chief of the village, stood with his arms folded, joking with the little children who ran around him. Wulfric was arguing with Golderon, his beautiful young wife, and grabbed her arm. She pulled away and stormed off to her house. It was a marriage arranged between their two fathers when Golderon was only fifteen, and not one that she was thankful for. Edwin could see his younger brother Edgar with his mother, Edith, sitting by the hot kiln with one of the Frisian traders from over the seas. The trader was a regular visitor, sailing from the continent and up the estuary of the Blackwater River to moor at Maldon, where he would deal in gold and semi-precious stones. Edith had become a very competent maker of jewellery, creating rings, brooches and necklaces. It was very unusual for a woman to be making these items.

Young Edwin cheerfully ambled along the ridge. But as his eyes wandered to the distant river estuary ahead of him, his mood changed and he suddenly froze. There, in the distance, unmistakeably, dozens of boats could be seen approaching the estuary.

'Oh no.'

Although they were still small to the eye, Edwin was in no doubt of what he was looking at. They were the longboats and sails of a huge force of an approaching Viking fleet. He felt his heart pounding and ran as fast as his legs would carry him towards the village, trying to keep hold of his catch. As he crossed the bridge over the ditch he shouted at the busy, bustling huts, and those within earshot stopped and stared. He was out of breath and could barely shout the words: 'The Heathens… Longboats… The Pagans are coming.' When they realised the words he was shouting, a general confusion set in and people immediately began appearing out of their houses.

Aldwine knew that, although this region of Essex had

been given to the Danes, who controlled the kingdom of East Anglia as part of the agreement Alfred had made with the Viking King Guthrum, here at Maldon, the Saxons had enjoyed relative independence and little interference from the Danes and the Vikings. However, a few ships may not be of any concern and may even pass them by.

Aldwine turned to his twelve-year-old son. 'How many ships do you think you saw, Edwin?'

'I don't know, Father… many… perhaps forty. Maybe more.'

Aldwine looked perplexed. This was a different matter. He spoke to the villagers around him. 'Such a large number of ships carry possibly over a thousand men, which could only mean one thing, and that is the return of Aethelwold with his Viking allies. It has been more than two years since he escaped the clutches of the King and now it seems he sailed south to the coast, where he knows the land belongs to the Pagans, and he has some support from the Viking communities who have settled here.'

The Saxon village had no hope of repelling such a large force.

'We have no choice but to submit to Aethelwold and recognise his Lordship.'

Groans were audible from some of the villagers, especially the women, as they feared that the Vikings, who brought few women with them, may demand sexual pleasures and even take them away.

'We will probably have to feed them and provide them with supplies. Luckily the harvest has given us good crops this last year and we have ample provisions.' And, quietly to Edwin standing beside him: 'I just hope they don't take it all.' He smiled, but his son could see the strain on his father's face.

The Vikings moored upriver and a large army of several hundred men disembarked and established a large camp next to the river. For a few days Cuthbert had left the village to scout around and later returned to the village to seek out Aldwine and inform him: 'Father, the Vikings are coming towards the village. There are many armed men.'

Aldwine took off his sword. He wanted the Vikings to know that he had no desire to cause any conflict. He went out over the bridge with a small retinue of six unarmed men who were the elders and council of Maldon.

The Vikings stopped short of the village and two men on horseback rode forward with a dozen foot soldiers carrying the battle pennants of their leaders. They halted in front of Aldwine. A large bearded man on a chestnut horse spoke first. 'I am Aethelwold, true King of the Saxons.' Then, pointing to the other man seated on a dapple-grey horse with a heavy cloak and surly look on his face: '...and this is Eohric, King of the Vikings in this region.'

Aldwine was rather taken aback. Aethelwold was no surprise, but he had gained the help of the East Anglian King Eohric, who had been given Essex and become its king when King Alfred had divided up England between the Saxon kingdom and the Danelaw.

'Er, g-greetings, King, we welcome you both to the town of Maldon and we accept you as our overlord and ruler.'

'I already am,' snarled Eohric sarcastically.

'Not if King Edward has anything to do with it,' Aldwine mumbled under his breath. Then, out loud: 'You will receive no opposition from us. We wish to live here in peace.'

'We need provisions, food for our troops. You will hand over your livestock. We need wheat, fruit, vegetables and honey.'

Wulfric, an aggressive and mean-looking man who was standing next to Aldwine, spluttered, 'You cannot take all our food – what about the people of our village?'

Aldwine glared at Wulfric. He knew he hated for the Vikings, but this was not the time to pick an argument with them.

Eohric rode forward and, taking off his glove, leant forward on his horse and slapped Wulfric around the face with it. 'Silence, dog. We will take what we want.'

Wulfric had a look of rage and resentment but knew there was nothing he could do.

Athelwold held up his hand as if to act as mediator. 'We will leave you plenty, never fear. But we have a long march and we need enough for at least the next few days. We will return with our carts in an hour.'

After they had returned, and continued on their way, much to Aldwine's relief, later that afternoon he gathered around him many of the men of the village to speak to them.

'Saxons, I am pleased to tell you that the Viking army has left the village and is on its way westwards.'

'Do you know where they are heading, Father?' enquired Edwin.

'No, but I expect they will go to the Wessex borderlands and raid the countryside there. But I have no doubt they intend ultimately to engage with King Edward and try to defeat him in battle.'

'And if he does?'

'Then Aethelwold will be King.' A look of dismay appeared on the faces of some of the villagers.

'However, their visit was not as bad as we expected. Believe me, it could have been a lot worse. They took no hostages and no women, which is what I was expecting. They have only a small number of our cows and sheep. No doubt larger numbers would have slowed up their march. We still have plenty of food. What is more, they failed to enlist hardly any men from the village to join their force. Of course, they could return and we need to be watchful. Also, to keep our eye out for more ships sailing up the river.' He looked at his son and smiled. He was very proud of Edwin, who had forewarned the village.

'Should we warn King Edward?'

'Oh yes, I have already sent out Cuthbert on horse to get ahead of the Vikings and try to find King Edward at Winchester. There, they should at least know of his whereabouts.' Aldwine knew he could trust his eldest son to get the message to the King Edward, as he was an accomplished rider and a good scout who would have a knack of being able to find his way.

WINCHESTER

Edward stood proudly before his new cathedral. This was the New Minster, bigger and grander than the old cathedral next to it. Grimbald, the architect whom Edward had commissioned to oversee its construction, had recently died and was already buried there before it was finished. Now it was complete. The nave was longer than the old minster with two floors but with more windows higher up in the entrance wall and two tall towers flanking the nave by the entrance. There was a large bell tower which sat at the centre of the nave. The bells were ringing out in memory of Edward's mother Elswitha, who had also just passed away. On the other side of New Minster was Nunnaminster, a new convent founded by Elswitha which Edward had completed in her name.

King Alfred's body was also to be moved from the old cathedral and interred into the New Minster so that Edward's parents could lie side by side. Two carriages, each pulled by a pair of black horses, moved slowly towards the entrance of the New Minster with their respective coffins. Edward's personal guard carried them into the Minster and they were laid either side of the chancel where Archbishop Plegmund conducted the Christian ceremony.

Afterwards in the Great Hall, everyone gathered for a celebration of the lives of Alfred and Elswitha. There were musicians in the north corner with a woman playing the lyre, a man playing a long horn and a young lad with his drum. A storyteller entertained the young children. A large feast was being prepared in the kitchen and the long table had been laid out for the royal contingent.

Edward's sister Athelflaed and her husband Ethelred, the Lord of Mercia, had travelled from the Mercian town of Gloucester where they had their palace. They were deep in conversation with the King in the anteroom off the hall.

'I am glad you have been able to make the journey today, Ethelred, especially as there have been reports of marauding Vikings that have penetrated into your lands.'

Ethelred was a short, thickset man with a bearded round face. He had many battle wounds from previous conflicts with the Vikings and he was a seasoned campaigner, leading the Mercians in many skirmishes against them. He was a confident man and a very able soldier.

'Yes, but only small bands of men mostly, and I have a big enough force to see them off. Perhaps with any luck I shall come across them upon my return.'

Edward chuckled. 'You seem to look forward to confronting our Danish neighbours, My Lord.'

Ethelred smiled a wicked smile. 'Edward…' there was a pause whilst Ethelred looked for the right words to put his proposal to the King, 'together we could have a great military alliance that could crush the Pagans and allow me to re-take the half of my kingdom which they presently occupy.'

'Yes, brother,' agreed Athelflaed, backing up her husband. 'We can continue our father's legacy and build defences along our frontiers.'

Edward nodded.

'Together, the kingdoms of Wessex and Mercia would indeed be a very powerful force. And there is no-one I could trust more than you, Ethelred.'

'Your sister has been a great help to me, Edward. And King Alfred's proposal for her to raise your son Athelstan in the Mercian Court would mean that one day our two families can be united in a common cause. Elfwyn is our only daughter and Athelflaed has been unable to have any more children. As we cannot have our son, Athelstan can inherit the Kingdom of Mercia and you have your younger son Alfweard who can inherit Wessex. He is only a baby now but hopefully will grow into a fine young man. As brothers, the next generation can continue the great alliance. But Elfwyn…?' Ethelred seem to rule out any inheritance by his daughter. 'This is a tough enough world for a man, let alone a woman.'

Athelflaed rolled her eyes and sighed.

Edward paced up and down. 'Mmm, but before we engage with the Pagans we have Aethelwold to deal with first. And we need to consolidate our position, improve our defences in our own towns and recruit more men for our army. Not to mention building more ships to combat those of the Vikings at sea.'

Later that day the family re-assembled in the Great Hall. Ethelred threw another log onto the fire. Edward entered with a young boy, just seven years old with a shock of blond hair and bright blue eyes. This was Athelstan, Edward's eldest son from his first marriage.

Athelstan greeted his Aunt Athelflaed and Ethelred. Edward looked a little uneasy. 'The time has now come, my son, for you to leave Winchester and join your aunt at the Mercian court at Gloucester. As we agreed.'

'Actually, we are going first to spend time at our modest palace at Worcester. We…'

He saw his wife glaring at him with a look that could kill and it stopped him short. Athelstan looked down at the floor. 'Yes. But… do I have to go right now, Father?' Tears began to well in his eyes, but he was determined not to cry in front of his father and his aunt and uncle.

'You know that it is difficult for me to look after you. Since your mother departed…'

Athelflaed knelt on the rug before Athelstan and took his hand. 'Do not fear, Athelstan, I will look after you. We have prepared some grand rooms for you at Gloucester, next to Elfwyn; she is looking forward to seeing you. The Bishop of Worcester will be your tutor, and he is one of the wisest and most clever men in the realm. You will learn much from him. Your uncle will teach you how to fight and ride.

The boy looked at his uncle. 'I can already ride my pony and I am already one of the best for my age with the sword.'

Ethelred chuckled. 'So I hear. You will be the best in all the kingdoms.'

Athelstan still felt tearful. He hugged his aunt.

At that moment Archbishop Plegmund appeared. 'A messenger, My Lord. He has ridden from the town of Maldon in the kingdom of Essex with news!'

'Show him in. More Pagan invaders, no doubt.'

The dishevelled horseman was closely escorted by the King's thegn into the room. The thegn had drawn his sword, as there was always a fear of a conspiracy and an assassination attempt. The messenger bowed before the King.

'I am Cuthbert from Maldon, Sire. I have been sent here to tell you that Athelwold has landed in Essex with many ships and he has with him Eohric, the Dane who claims to be overlord there.'

'Ah so he makes an appearance at last, does he? How many men?'

'Several hundred, Sire, but he is scouring the Danish and Viking villages and persuading their men to join him.'

Edward glanced at Ethelred. 'I see. I wonder where he is heading.'

Ethelred stroked his beard 'I will prepare a Mercian force and head for Oxford. From there we will send out scouts to keep track of his route.'

'Good. I will send a message to Sigehelm and his Kentish men to make their way north. We need reinforcements from them and since my father made me King of Kent they have pledged their loyalty to me. They are a good fighting force. Once we rendezvous with them, our combined army will wreak havoc in East Anglia and engage with Athelwold if we can find him.'

'I can ride to Kent for you, Sire,' volunteered Cuthbert, although he was feeling very tired. He was anxious to please the King.

'No, no, Cuthbert, I will send my team of armed messengers.' He beckoned to one of his assistants. 'Make sure this man is given plenty of food and drink. Give him a fresh horse. But you must rest, Cuthbert, and when you return to Essex I ask you to come back with any men that wish to support us and able to fight for our cause. And I thank you for bringing us this news.'

'It is an honour, Lord.' And as Cuthbert left, Edward picked up little Athelstan with fondness – it was going to be hard for him too, he was going to see much less of his eldest son. 'Time for you to go, my son. Be an obedient servant to your aunt and uncle. Learn much and don't forget that one day you will be King.'

Athelflaed took the young prince by the hand and made arrangements to depart. Edward prepared once again to mobilise his men.

PETERBOROUGH (MEDESHAMSTEDE)

The cold December rain had been steady for hours and the light was already beginning to fade. They arrived at twilight at a town by the side of a monastery which looked in a very poor state of ruin and almost deserted, although in the part of the monastery that remained a candlelight could be seen from one of the upper windows.

'It is time to make camp. What is this place, Athelweard?'

'It is the town of Medeshamstede, brother, but some call it Peterborough. It is still part of Ethelred's kingdom but a little further east we cross into East Anglia. It was from there that in your father's reign, the Vikings raided the town, sacking the monastery and murdering the abbot and his monks.'

A steely growl came from the King, who muttered words nobody could hear. 'This is why I hate the Pagans, brother. Heathens who plunder our Saxon villages and towns and put to death, sometimes in a vile way, innocent godly men, men of peace who would do no harm but intend only to spread the word of Christ. I am determined to one day unite these kingdoms into one Christian land.'

The army set out their tents and prepared for supper. The King, after his meal, decided to take his usual stroll around the camp to talk to his men. As he walked into the chill night, he could see the candlelight burning outside the tents and approached two men huddled around a small fire trying to keep warm. He instantly recognised one of them.

'Cuthbert. I am glad to see you here.'

Cuthbert beamed. He was impressed that the King had remembered his name. 'My Lord King. This is my younger brother Edwin.'

Edwin was rather dumbstruck and bowed to the King.

'Greetings, Edwin. How old are you?' The King could see a fine youth before him, but he seemed barely out of boyhood.

'Fifteen, Sire.'

'Mmm. So young for a fighting soldier. I hope you will look after him, Cuthbert.'

'Oh yes, he does, Sire… well, we look after each other.' He placed his hand on Edwin's shoulder.

The King smiled and went to walk away but stopped and turned.

'I think there will be no more fighting this year anyway.' Edward had come to a sudden decision.

'Oh?'

'We have harried the Vikings and sent them packing. But it is winter and the season will get even colder. It is time to return home.'

'Yes, but what of Athelwold, My Lord?'

'The scouts have just returned and they have not been able to locate his army at present. We can try again in the spring. Say nothing to anyone. I still have to break the news to the thegns and the ealdormen. Good to see you both.'

'Of course, My Lord.' The brothers looked at each other as the King departed.

'Looks like we are back to Maldon tomorrow, brother.' Edwin shrugged.

The King had gathered the leaders of the army and his travelling council into his large tent and told them of his intention to return to Winchester without delay. Sigehelm, who was the ealdorman who commanded the large

Kent fyrd and a tough if ageing old campaigner, was not particularly happy with the decision to part.

'Surely we can still find Athelwold and the Viking army and crush them! We have enough men and some of Ethelred's army lies to the west.'

'Nothing more I would like better, but we could be a long time searching and they may have returned to Northumbria for all we know. No, we have been out on campaign for long enough; it is time to return to our families, who will no doubt be pleased to see us. In any case, our time is nearly due. The way my father organised the army was clever and commendable: three divisions, one would stay at home and rest for six months and only be called in an emergency whilst another was on duty to campaign and fight wherever they were needed. A third were allocated to defend the bergs. Our six months are nearly up. I am heading back west and you should take your men south back to Kent, Sigehelm.'

Sigehelm scowled. 'We will stay a while, maybe harass the Danes to the east until the end of the month or until the weather deteriorates.'

'Go back to Kent, Sigehelm. In time to celebrate Yule. I thank you for your support and hope you have a safe journey back.'

A few days later, Edward was back with his men into the safety of Saxon territory. Cuthbert, who had gone with the King, had now been employed as scout and was in charge of a small squad of four men, including his younger brother. He had already been sent back to see if the Kent men had returned south only to find them still camped in the same spot, driving them eastwards and raiding the countryside where the Danes could be found. He reported to the King.

Eventually, Sigehelm reluctantly struck camp and started to head back on the road south toward Kent. It was bright and sunny but there was a keen and bitter wind. A few hours later Sigehelm was moving his army uphill when his scout approached at speed. He reached Sigehelm, breathless.

'Viking army coming this way, heading straight for us!'

'Is there now? Well, well. Let me see for myself.' He beckoned to his personal bodyguards to accompany him to the top of the hill. There he was a little surprised to see just how close the Vikings were. And marching towards him at speed. The Kent men were drastically outnumbered, probably, Sigehelm calculated, by two to one.

'Oh, to hell with them. We'll fight. Show them that the men of Kent are no pushovers.' Sigehelm realised that there wasn't really much choice. No doubt he had already been spotted and the Vikings blocked their way home. There was little chance of escape considering the short distance between them. To his left and slightly ahead of him was some higher ground. He took his men off the road and formed his men into a long line across the ridge with their round shields touching man to man. The baggage train and the thegns were behind with Sigehelm.

The Vikings began to form up at the foot of the slope and a contingent raced by them along the road northwards.

'To cut off our retreat,' Sigehelm said to his second in command Uhtred. He surveyed what was in front of him. He could just make out the banners of the leaders of the Pagan army. Athelwold and Eohric to the right side of their troops sat on horses behind a pond with a copse of trees and thick undergrowth to their right flank. An idea immediately struck Sigehelm, but he must act quickly. He told of his plan to Uhtred, who would take command of the men in front of him whilst a dozen of his horsemen would ride with him back down the slope and detour around the trees. He and his men rode fast behind the cover of the woods as the Viking army, banging their shields and shouting their war cries, suddenly advanced rapidly up towards the Saxon shield wall.

Athelwold looked on as the Vikings with overwhelming numbers crashed into the Saxon army. But suddenly he was aware that horsemen had appeared almost behind him and he recognised Sigehelm amongst a band of mounted men coming at him. Sigehelm tried to come around Athelwold so that he was wedged between his men and the thick undergrowth. With the pond in front there was nowhere to go, and Athelwold, Eodhric and their personal retinue turned to fight. A large body of Viking footmen to the left realised what was happening and ran to try to help their leaders. Sigehelm and two of his men slashed at Eodhric with their swords. The Viking fell from his horse, but with his foot caught in the leather stirrup, as his frightened horse galloped away, Eodhric's bloody body was dragged along the ground. Three more Saxon horsemen had cornered Athelwold, but the Viking soldiers rushed into the affray and overpowered Sigehelm, dragging him from his horse. A Viking thrust a sword deep into him. The last thing Sigehelm saw was Athelwold's body floating face down in the shallow pond with a spear protruding from his back and his wooden shield floating next to him.

Up on the hill the vast numbers of the Vikings at

last overwhelmed the Saxon army, who broke and fled as fast as they could down into the woods and the thick undergrowth. A few of the Vikings made chase, but word had spread quickly that their kings had both been killed, and the deflated soldiers, now leaderless, were in no mood to prolong the fighting.

A few hours later Cuthbert and Edwin were trotting down the road south from Peterborough, having seen the Saxon men were no longer in camp, and suddenly appeared on the battlefield to find a scene of devastation in front of them. 'What hell is this, brother?' Bodies lay all around. The tiny Saxon community of Holme, half a mile away, which consisted of an extended family group of twenty, were taking away the Saxon bodies on a cart to give them a Christian burial, although Cuthbert suspected that some looting of the bodies had already taken place. He spoke with one of them, who gave him a report of the battle.

'Are those Danish soldiers over there?' Edwin pointed to the distant horizon, where a large band of men were huddled around a fire outside their tents, trying to keep warm.

'Yes, but they won't bother you. They have no stomach to fight.' And he explained that the leaders of both sides had fallen in the battle.

'Come, Edwin, we need to report immediately to the King.'

WINCHESTER

At the Great Hall King Edward was in the anteroom with Archbishop Plegmund and the Bishop of Winchester. He was checking the final draft of a charter which allocated land to Ealdorman Aethelfrith, a loyal subject who had paid money to acquire church lands in Buckinghamshire.

'I will sign it as "*King of the Saxons*". If you can arrange a council meeting in the spring, please, Archbishop, then we can get the lords and members of the council to sign this and the other outstanding charters. We need then to arrange a meeting with Ethelred and my sister to discuss and work out the burghal hidage. My father has built many fortifications in Wessex, but we need to extend these to our borderlands and one day beyond into the Danelaw, which I intend to conquer and protect the Saxon population there.' The archbishop bowed, rolled up the charter and left the room. Edward strolled out into the Great Hall, throwing a log onto the fire, where a large chicken was roasting on a spit. He greeted his brother and his wife, who had just entered the hall, and kissed his wife Aelfflaed, whom he joined on the long table. She was once again heavily pregnant. The servants entered to serve up a hearty meal.

Meanwhile, Cuthbert and Edwin rode into the courtyard and dismounted, quickly making their way to the Great Hall. The personal bodyguard at the door stepped in front of them. 'The King is at supper. You need to wait.'

'The King will not want to wait for important news I have for him.'

'Well, that is for the King to decide.'

'Oh, just let me talk to him.'

'But…'

'It's alright, let him enter.'

Athelweard, who faced the door, noticed the commotion and nudged his brother. 'It's Cuthbert, back with news. He looks agitated.'

Cuthbert and Edwin bowed before the Royal family.

'So what news, Cuthbert? Did you find Sigehelm?'

'Yes, Lord, he has been killed in a battle with the Vikings. But—'

'Oh no!' Edward put his head in his hands. 'I might have known. He was always looking to go too far. Too ambitious. Too much hate for his enemy.'

'But—'

'I told him to return. How many times? Now he has paid the price. He—'

'*But, My Lord!*' Edwin raised his voice, almost shouting. Athelweard glared at him.

'Aethelwold has been slain also. He is dead, My Lord.'

There was a stunned few seconds' silence.

'Really?' The King stood up, throwing his chicken bone onto the plate.

'Yes, Sire, and dead also is Eohric, the Danish King.'

Athelweard smiled at his brother. He slammed his fist onto the table. 'Excellent. The threat we have suffered these last few years has been removed.'

Edward's wife hugged her husband.

'I owe the men of Kent a large debt. I hope they don't feel that I abandoned Sigehelm.' Edward turned to his brother. 'You know, Athelweard, if only my cousin had come to me and accepted me as king, he would have become a very powerful noble and I could have made him ruler in East Anglia once we had reinstated the lands there to Saxon rule.'

'And if anything happened to you, he probably would have succeeded as king.'

Edward raised his eyebrows. 'I would have thought you

would have had a claim, brother.'

Athelweard smiled. 'I think I am destined for the Church and have no wish to be king. I am not sure I could do a good job of it. Though I very much doubt Aethelwold would have made a good king either. You are the right man for the job, brother.'

'Nevertheless, loyal brother, if anything happens to me, God forbid, you are next in line. Which is why I would like you to control things here in Winchester, when I am out on campaign against the Pagans.'

Athelweard nodded in acceptance. There was glory in fighting in battle, but he had a family now. And what the King said made sense.

'And as for you, Cuthbert and Edwin, a reward of a new horse each, I think. I have just acquired some beautiful new stallions.'

The two brothers were puffed up with pride.

'I feel a poem coming on,' said Athelweard.

'"*Slain by the men of Kent was the traitor Athelwold.*

'"*The King's messenger was rewarded in gold.*"

'See. It rhymes.'

The ladies laughed, the scouting brothers chuckled and the King smiled.

'I feel relieved.' He sighed. 'Now we can turn our attention to other matters.'

CHAPTER 4
THE YEAR 906
GLOUCESTER

Ethelred and Athelflaed sat at the table in their royal house with Athelstan sat between them. Stood before them was Helvin, who had arrived from the Wirral in the far north of their kingdom.

'Sit, Helvin.' Ethelred gestured to the chair opposite them. 'What brings you here?'

'Well, My Lord and Lady, unfortunately it seems Ingimund is intent on causing you trouble.'

'Oh?'

'He has desires to seize Chester for himself. He has persuaded the other Viking chieftains to go along with it. The Danes are fully supportive, although the Norwegians are not so keen.'

Athelflaed looked at her husband and frowned. 'Damnation. What a nerve. We had the decency to allow his Pagan clan to settle in the Wirral after being expelled from Dublin by the Irish. Now he wants to betray us and take our town.'

'I think that's what is called getting too big for your boots.' Ethelred sighed. 'When is he planning to carry this out?'

'In about a week, Lord, maybe a little longer.'

'It will take nearly a week to march our army there.'

Athelflaed groaned. 'Yes, but with much effort I can get there in five days, and arrive before the attack takes place.'

'I don't think the town are aware of his plans.'

'We can warn the townsfolk and the local fyrd. Thank you, Helvin, you have done well. The cook will give you a meal and I will arrange for your reward of silver coin. Does Ingimund have any suspicion of your trip here?'

'I don't believe so, My Lady. I told everyone I was visiting my Mercian relations.' Helvin bowed and left the room.

Ethelred turned to his wife. 'Good idea of yours to plant Helvin in the Viking camp and provide us with information about Ingimund's movements.'

'Yes, he has been useful. I chose him because although he has a Norwegian father, his mother is a Mercian. His family wishes the Vikings and the Saxon nation to get along.'

'Is Chester an important town, Uncle?'

'Yes, Athelstan, it acts as a sort of lookout post because it sits on the border with the Welsh kingdoms and also lies between the Rivers Dee and Mersey where the Vikings from Ireland seem to choose to navigate when they come to England. In fact, much trade occurs between Chester and Ireland. There are Irish and Viking people who live there but the Saxon reeve and the ealdorman there have always been loyal to us.' He turned to his wife. 'Well, my dear, if you prepare our men and leave as soon as possible, I will stay behind and look after things here, as my health is not so good these days. I will also send a message to Edward to let him know what is happening.'

Athelflaed nodded. 'I will travel by way of Worcester on the way and request that my good friend Bishop Werferth accompany me north. I intend to build a new church in the town and dedicate it to St Peter but build a shrine within to St Werburgh. She was the daughter of a Mercian king and an inspiration to Christianity. Two hundred years ago, her body was carried through the town. The bishop can consecrate the new church.'

'May I go with you, Aunt?' Athelstan looked hopeful.

'I am not sure that is such a good idea.'

'You should take him, dearest. Let him see how we operate.'

'I am twelve now, Aunt, nearly thirteen.'

Athelflaed laughed. 'Okay, but against my better judgement. You must to stick close by me at all times, Athelstan.'

CHESTER (LEGECEASTERSCIR)

Athelflaed gazed down at the River Dee. The rustic autumn colours were at their very best, but a strengthening breeze was taking the leaves away from the trees that lined the river. She was a handsome lady rather than beautiful, with high cheekbones and strawberry-blonde hair which was almost onto her shoulders, but she did not allow it to get any longer for practical reasons. She was a little taller than the average Saxon woman and had the family trait of a slender but wiry body. She had her usual steely look of determination, but although she was weary after the long journey with her Mercian army which was camped within the town, she knew that time was of the essence and she needed to oversee the defences of Chester, which had the remains of the old Roman fortifications. For the time being she would do the best she could to get her subjects to shore up the old defences and plug any holes or restore any weakness in the walls. Bishop Werferth was showing Athelstan around the existing churches in the town.

Once the makeshift defences were complete Athelflaed called her thegns together to discuss their strategy and tactics as to how they would fight the Pagans. They didn't have long to wait. The next day scouts from the Wirral to the north reported the approaching Danish army. Athelflaed commanded her two most prominent thegns to take a small contingent of handpicked Saxon warriors to establish a position in front of the town gates, forming a long line of men ending on the west side at the banks of the River Dee.

The invaders rapidly advanced on foot towards the Saxon line. Athelflaed stood with Athelstan and Werferth on the walkway above the town gates to watch the events. The Danes clashed with the Saxon warriors, who held fast for a while, although outnumbered. Athelflaed signalled to her herald to sound the horn. The gates were opened and the Saxons broke from the attack, running as fast as they could back into the town. They were pursued by Ingrimund's Vikings, who were only able to catch a small number of the Saxons before they poured through the gates.

Once inside, the Saxon men raced towards another line of Saxon men standing with gaps between them. As they reached the line they turned to face their foes, filling the gaps and raising their shields to form a wall. Spears were let loose towards the surprised attackers. In the meantime, a large body of Saxon horsemen appeared from behind the gates, which were hastily closed, and began to hew with swords from both sides of the now-beleaguered Danish force.

The Saxon line of foot soldiers then moved forward and Athelstan watched wide-eyed as the whole Heathen force was struck down from all sides until virtually every one of them lay dead in the town. A number of invaders, who had remained outside the walls and refrained from taking part in the attack, turned and disappeared. Athelflaed ordered her men to remove the bodies to outside the town walls, where they would be buried in a mass grave, but requested her thegns to try to locate the body of Ingrimund.

'He does not seem to be here, My Lady.'

'Mmm, he lives to fight another day maybe. But I doubt he will be back to Chester in a hurry.'

'The Danish Vikings are very unpopular here, My Lady. But what about the Norwegians, some of whom already live within the town and have remained neutral over this matter?' enquired Bishop Werferth.

'I cannot trust them. Ask them to leave. Yes, they must go, and if they refuse they will be thrown out by force.'

'Also we have captured outside the gates a badly wounded man called Ronan, who is one of the Irish leaders. Do you wish him to be executed, My Lady?'

'No! Call the medical men to see to him. I would like to have a conversation with this man.'

Ronan, a short red-haired man, was brought before Athelflaed and Athelstan, looking pale and tired and heavily bandaged. He bowed to his conqueror but requested that he could sit as he was feeling very weak.

'Yes, of course.' She beckoned for him to be given a chair. 'I understand you should be able to make a recovery from your wounds?'

'Yes, Lady Athelflaed. I thank you for the attention of your medical men who have shown me kindness.'

'You know of my name then?'

Ronan looked surprised. 'Why, yes. You are well known both in Ireland and the Wirral.'

'I am glad you feel better. Naturally I have a motive for my actions.'

Ronan afforded a weak smile. 'I had anticipated as much.'

'The thing is, you are a Christian, are you not?'

Ronan nodded. 'Of course.'

'Then why do you side with the Pagans against us?'

'They paid us. And promised us access to Chester. To be honest, we have no affinity with the Danes. Actually, Ingrimund is a very unpleasant man.'

'Well, consider this. I will pay you double whatever the Vikings offered. But I will also allow the Irish into Chester. You can have your own quarter. I intend to re-fortify it and extend the streets to provide more houses.'

'And in exchange?'

'Slay these Vikings and send them into hell. We can be allies, united by our Christian faith.'

Ronan smiled and looked at Athelflaed but said nothing as if he was contemplating the idea.

'And we have spared your life.'

'And what guarantees can you give us?'

'I will pay you half the money now and provide you with hostages. But you must keep them safe and release them when you return to Chester.'

'You have a reputation of honesty, My Lady. So I will talk with my fellow leaders and make plans to carry out this task.' Ronan staggered to his feet and made his way out. Athelflaed winked at Athelstan, who smiled broadly. His aunt was clever but could also be quite devious when she wanted.

Athelflaed stayed in Chester with Athelstan and Werferth for some weeks. Athelflaed wanted to see the finished church with the shrine that she dedicated to St Werburgh and the renewed fortification and the repair of the Roman walls of the town.

'I will organise a rota with Saxon sentries on duty day and night, Bishop,' she declared to Werferth. 'This is the strategy my father adopted in Wessex and one which Edward and I intend to follow.'

'And it seems to work, My Lady. Incidentally, I have news about Ingrimund's invading Heathen force. It appears that, as you had planned, the Christian Irish levies in his army successfully rebelled against the Heathens, tricking them into disarming and then killing them.'

'Oh. And what of Ingrimund?'

'Well, unfortunately it seems he managed to escape once again. But we are not sure whether it was back to his camp in the Wirral or elsewhere. I doubt he returned to Ireland.'

'Mmm. Anyway, I think Athelstan and I can return to Gloucester now. I am happy with the defences here and I am confident the townsfolk can repel a Pagan attack. If the Irish appear we will give instructions to allow them into the town.'

CHAPTER 5
THE YEAR 908
MALDON

This news was not good. Aldwine and Edwin looked solemn. A bedraggled and tearful teenage Saxon girl sat before them. 'You are Golderon's younger sister, aren't you?'

The girl nodded. 'Yes, Mildryth.'

'So, Mildryth, you say this Viking force landed early yesterday morning at Bradwell, sacked the church and stole its treasures. Then they dragged off your brother, er, Galan, and murdered your father?'

'Yes,' blubbered Mildryth. 'I could only watch helplessly as they took Galan away onto one of their longships. I do not know what will happen to him. He is only twelve. Then they ran a sword right through my poor father in front of my eyes.'

'You knew him, didn't you, Father?'

'Yes. Our two families go back a long way. A fine man from a noble family. They went out to start their own farming community at Bradwell several years ago. And so then you fled Mildryth?'

She nodded. 'We just ran as fast as we could to get away from them.'

'Well, you came to the right place. About two hundred men, you say. Well, we have no choice but to fight them. It's a day's march to Bradwell, unless we sail down the Blackwater. Mmm, let me think. There again, I don't relish meeting up with Viking longships on the water. I feel we would be safer on land. We need three hundred able-bodied men at least. Edwin, with Cuthbert still with the King I am relying on you to ride out to the little community at Totham and then to Witham to see if you can enlist a few more men. We cannot afford to wait too long. They probably intend to plunder the countryside.'

'Yes, Father, I will see what I can do.' Edwin was now twenty-one years old and a fine, strong young man. He mounted his horse. Edgar, his younger brother, tried to comfort poor Mildryth and put his arm around her shoulder.

The next day Edwin was able to return with forty men. The Saxons planned to leave early the next day. It was late spring so the days were long. If they left soon after sunrise they could arrive at Bradwell by midday. Aldwine would accompany them but Wulfric would lead the men into battle.

Edwin was old enough to fight too, whilst his youngest son, Edgar, would stay at home.

Aldwine turned to Edwin. 'We don't have as many men as I would have liked. You can lead a brigade of our two dozen horsemen, Edwin.'

'We can try and pick up a few more men from the villages along the way, Father.'

'These Vikings are chance prospectors, but it sounds like they are aggressive and are not prepared to negotiate. They obviously have nothing to do with the East Anglian Danes. King Edward has just signed a peace treaty with them at Tiddingford. They must be a different contingent.'

'We must do what we can to defend our land, Father.'

Early the following morning the Maldon fyrd prepared for the march to Bradwell. Edith appeared with a cloak for her son and a brooch she had made to pin the cloak together. The brooch was made of bronze and semi-precious stones, and the colours of blue and gold matched Edwin's shield. She pulled the cloak around Edwin's shoulders. 'I hope this brooch is a lucky one. Be careful and don't be too reckless.' She turned to Aldwine. 'Look out for him, husband.' There was an anxious look on her face.

'Do not fret, my dear. He is very capable. I think it will be him looking out for me, not the other way around.'

Edith watched the party as they set out. Aldwine and Wulfric led the army of about two hundred men and Edwin alongside with his horsemen. At the rear was a wagon with tents and food and a few women including Wulfric's beautiful wife Golderon, whom he had insisted must come along, plus a few carts carrying more men but which would be used to take away the dead and wounded if it came to that.

At Latchingdon the army picked up a dozen more men, but when they reached Tillingham a few hours later, they found the houses of the little family group there burnt to the ground and a Saxon man hanging from a tree. Edwin seethed. Aldwine appeared alongside him. 'This is what they do. How do you deal with it? The King's strategy is to give them a dose of the same unless they submit to him and recognise them as King. But even then…'

Shortly after, they approached the tents around the chapel at Bradwell, but the Viking scouts must have seen them earlier and there were two long lines of Vikings standing ready, so there was to be no surprise attack. And it seemed, no intention to negotiate as the Vikings shouted and shook their spears and axes at the oncoming Saxons.

Aldwine, who knew the area well, ordered them to swing to the north and sent a band of thirty men to line up behind a ditch. The rest marched along the track and formed up into a dense shield wall. Arrows and spears were thrown on both sides and then, with a battle cry, both sides advanced into one another, clashing shields. Hacking and thrusting with swords, axes and spears, the two sides fought ferociously for some twenty minutes. Suddenly, behind them a band of about thirty Viking warriors appeared, coming along the track the Saxons had come along. They were led by a Viking warrior over six feet tall, who must have come from a boat at Pewet Island to the north. Edwin spotted the danger and tried to cut off the advancing Vikings, sending his horsemen towards them. A dozen Vikings got through and some of the Saxons were attacked from behind. The tall Viking cut down Wulfric with a massive blow from his axe. A horn sounded and the Saxon line broke and ran back towards the men behind the ditch. Edwin's horsemen harassed the chasing Vikings, successfully stopping the leading men and then galloping back to the ditch, which some hurdled over. A little planked crossing was quickly removed once all the Saxons were across and the Viking men came to a standstill on the opposite side of the ditch facing their Saxon foes, but they realised to try and cross the ditch would be suicidal. It was a stand-off. The Vikings eventually withdrew.

Dozens of men from both sides lay dead and dying. Aldwine realised that the wagons and carts had been captured by the late-arriving Vikings along with Golderon, whom they had tied to the wagon and then bound her hands behind her back. She was being guarded by the tall Viking, who appeared to want her for himself.

'What now, Father?'

'Sit and wait.'

Aldwine was going to stay there with his army, hoping to make the Pagans feel uneasy. They might, he thought, be expecting Saxon reinforcements. The Pagan soldiers watched them from a short distance. Time ticked by.

Sure enough, after an hour's wait, a small party appeared.

Three Vikings, two leaders of the raiding force and the six-foot warrior who had held Golderon stepped forward.

'I am Olaf, leader of these men. We are claiming this land and wish to settle here.'

Aldwine was used to Vikings visiting and even settling on their land, but he did not like the look of Olaf, who appeared shifty and cunning. 'We have no objection to this in principle. But why do you plunder the land and murder the local people?'

'They attacked us first and we defended ourselves.'

Aldwine knew this was a lie. He decided to call Olaf's bluff. 'Saxon reinforcements are on their way to us as we speak. However, we will not oppose your settlement on certain conditions.'

The Viking leader gave him a wary look.

'You return our carts so that we can take away our dead and give them a Christian burial.'

'Agreed. Bury them in the name of your Christian God and your precious… Jesus if that is what you believe.'

'Cease any further ravaging or devastation of this land.'

'Agreed.' A slight pause. 'Providing they do not attack us first, of course.'

Aldwine did not trust his adversary over this matter.

'And give back Golderon, the Saxon woman you have enslaved, so that she can return to her village.'

Olaf smirked sarcastically. 'I doubt if you would be able to prise her from Gerth.' Edwin's look was one of dismay.

The giant Viking said nothing but shook his head. The three men hesitated but then, feeling any further conversation over the matter would be useless, they backed away and returned to their men.

Aldwine ordered his dead warriors to be piled up on the carts and began back towards Maldon. It would be dark by the time they got back.

'What can we do about Golderon, Father?'

Aldwine looked at his son. 'You have an affection for her, I see. But for the moment there is little we can do. We will have to bide our time and consider carefully how to get her back. Her husband has been killed in the battle.'

'I doubt if she mourns for him, Father. Their marriage was arranged by the fathers of their respective families and Golderon was persuaded into it, but she never loved Wulfric.'

Aldwine looked thoughtful. 'No. He was a difficult man to love, I imagine.'

As they continued to journey back home, Edwin took his cloak slung over his horse and wrapped it around him. He went to fasten it with his brooch when he suddenly realised that his brooch was missing. He stopped to hold out the cloak in front of him to see if it was caught in it somehow. He looked on the ground around him.

'What's wrong, Edwin?'

'My new brooch, that Mother made for me. It looks like I have lost it.'

'It must have become unattached when you led your charge into the melee with the Vikings.'

Edwin felt extremely deflated. His mother had spent many hours forging this brooch for him. When he arrived back, he went straight to his house where Edith was cooking. She turned when she heard him enter and felt great relief to see him in one piece, immediately throwing her arms around him.

'Mother, my brooch… I have lost it. I feel terrible.'

'Oh. Never mind, Edwin, I am just happy they you have returned alive. Have you any injuries?'

'No, I am fine. Hardly a scratch on me.'

'Then that is all that matters. I can make you another brooch. Where is your father?'

'On the way. He is fine too.'

'Thank God. Tell me what happened.'

Edgar entered the house and gave his brother a friendly punch. 'Pleased to see you, brother.'

Edith provided them both with a bowl of food as Edwin began to tell his account of the day's events. At the end, he questioned his father. 'How do you know Golderon's family then?'

'Why, my great-grandfather and her ancestor virtually founded this village. Almost a hundred years ago my grandfather farmed this area. One day, so the story goes, he walked up to the top of the hill with Golderon's ancestor, his farming neighbour, where we are now, and they found that someone had mysteriously placed a ten-foot-high wooden cross in the ground at the top of the hill. It was a time when Viking raiders were coming to this area for the first time and they realised that the top of the hill by the cross was a very good defensive position where they may be able to protect themselves against the Pagan plunderers. The land rose steeply on the south side of the River Blackwater, though there was a more gentle slope to the east. Also there was a good track to the west which joined with the old Roman roads. They were both enthusiastic about creating a small community and invited their extended family of brothers and sisters to come and build their houses.

'They also built our small wooden chapel by the cross over the next several years and my grandfather proposed a watermill, but this was half a mile further to the west on the River Chelmer, which, as you know, is a tributary of the Blackwater, forking off on its south side.

'As the raids increased in frequency, more families from further afield asked if they could join us. We created a wooden palisade around the town and slowly the village developed. Now look at how it has grown. My grandfather and father became leader of the village, but Golderon's father married a Bradwell girl and he went off to expand her farms out there and decided to stay. His wife died, but

I kept in touch with him ever since. I can't believe he has been taken from us. I will pray for him and his family.'

WINCHESTER

As it was a warm spring day, Edward sat outside the royal house in the courtyard. Plegmund came striding over with a scroll of vellum under his arm looking somewhat perplexed.

'Lord, would you have any objection to creating new bishops in the Diocese of Wessex? I am struggling with the administration of our kingdom. Asser and Denewulf are very helpful but Asser is very elderly now and not a well man.'

'You work very hard, Archbishop. What did you have in mind?'

'I was thinking of three new bishops creating a see in Crediton for Devon and Cornwall, Ramsbury for Wiltshire and Wells for Somerset.'

'Wouldn't you need permission from the pontiff to approve such new offices?'

'Yes, My Lord. I would have to write to the current Bishop of Rome, Sergius III, outlining my proposals.'

Edward thought for a moment. 'You know, Archbishop, my father visited Rome when he was a boy, but we have not had an archbishop from Canterbury visit Rome for decades – over a hundred years, I think. What do you think about the idea of travelling there yourself?'

'Well, that would be a trip.' Plegmund's eyes lit up.

'You can leave things here to Asser and Denewulf. Take a few young priests of potential with you and return in a few months.'

'I would love to see Rome, My Lord. What a splendid idea.'

'Yes, it could be quite an adventure. You could journey to Sandwich and cross the Channel and then hire horses to ride down through the Kingdom of the Franks, stopping overnight until you reach Rome.'

'I will make the necessary preparations and leave at the end of next week. Thank you, My Lord.'

Edward smiled. 'Keep me informed. Oh, would you tell my brother I will be spending time at the Royal House at King's Worthy?'

Although Edward retained his father's Royal Lodge at Kings Worthy, two miles north of Winchester, he spent most of his time at his home by the New Minster. The palace had used the old stone wall of the Roman walls as the east wall. This bordered onto the River Itchen. The rest of the building – or, to be accurate, buildings, as there were many outbuildings – were of wooden structure with a high thatched roof. The main hall was built of stone and had a stone floor and a central fireplace and a gap in the ceiling to let the smoke out. Around it were five tall, comfortable chairs with cushions. A long dining table was placed in the centre of the hall with benches all the way along and the King's chair was at the head of the table. Gold-threaded tapestries adorned the walls. At the east end and separated by wooden walls was the King's bedchamber on one side and the children's rooms on the other. The King had a sumptuous feather bed with lots of cushions. Rugs adorned the floor. Alongside the King's room, built on as an afterthought, were two guest bedrooms. Between the two was a smaller room which was the latrine; it contained a gap in the Roman wall where everything could be deposited into the river.

At the other end of the Great Hall was a room built onto the south side which was the kitchen, with its tables, large hanging cauldrons and pans, an oven for baking bread and another fireplace which was a circular stone pit with a spit. Pales of water were placed nearby, as accidents with kitchen fires were commonplace. At the west end were the servants' quarters. The main door was on the south side and a path ran around to the west side and the huge courtyard. Across the other side were the two minsters, old and new.

Near to the King's room, on the north side, was a room which nobody was allowed to enter without permission. It remained locked and only the King, or his clerk and the Bishop of Winchester, had keys to the door. Just outside in the hall was a cupboard which contained an assortment of candles and silver candlesticks. Inside there was a cupboard with scrolls and writing quills, a desk and a round table and chairs. Also there were two large chests containing treaties and charters of great value. They were neat scrolls of parchment containing agreements with Scots and the Welsh, some of his European neighbours and Viking kings. Other documents contained charters giving land titles to noblemen and town charters authorising coin mints, various churches to be built and other such lawful decrees.

Also on the north side of the palace, outside, was the orchard. They called it the apple orchard but there were pear and plumb trees as well. Next to the orchard was the kitchen garden, which grew all sorts of vegetables and a variety of herbs. Also a strawberry patch, one of the King's favourites. Beyond the orchard, but still within the town walls, was the royal farm, which kept just a few pigs and chickens for the King's dinner but was constantly being replenished from the main farm near Kings Worthy. Here were cattle and sheep as well as a large lake stocked with fish such as carp. Next to the royal farm was the Winchester watermill on the River Itchen. The wheel turned to make the flour for the bread needed every day by the town's population.

On the south side were various outbuildings, including the stables where the King's white stallion lived. Nearby were two large buildings, built from the old Roman stone, always locked and heavily guarded. One was the armoury, containing rows of swords, spears axes and shields. Next to it stood the treasury, filled with gold and silver coin, and a variety of valuable ornaments such as challises and crown jewels being prepared for display.

To the west, the large towers of the New Minster threw long shadows across the courtyard towards the palace, and beyond the minsters and also to the south of the hall were the crowded houses of Winchester, fast becoming one of the largest cities in England.

It was late afternoon when Athelflaed entered the hall at Winchester with her husband Ethelred and her nephew Athelstan. The King was very pleased to see them and overjoyed at the sight of his eldest son, whom he embraced first. He was now fourteen years old and the Prince – or aetheling, as the sons of the kings were called – was growing into a fine young man.

'How was your journey from Gloucester?'

'Long!' Ethelred looked tired and frail. Now elderly in his sixties, he had exceeded the age most men lived in Saxon England.

Edward smiled and slapped Ethelred on the back. 'Well, good of you to come, but I need you here for good reason. I want to discuss with you, and my sister and my brother, the future of our kingdoms and the way forward. Where is your daughter?'

'Elfwyn stays behind in Gloucester. Her preference is for learning and contemplation for pious matters.'

'Well, our debate can wait. For now you must eat and rest.'

After dinner, while most rested in their chambers, Athelstan sat by the fire with his father. As dark descended, the candles were lit and the King looked with satisfaction at his son. 'You realise that I want you to attend our family meeting tomorrow, don't you?'

'Thank you. I would like that.'

'You still have much to learn but you will soon be ready to fight for the Saxon cause.'

'When did you first fight against the Danes, Father?'

'Well, when I was eleven I didn't fight, but I joined my father when we marched to Rochester, where a Danish force had set up defences. But when we got there, they fled to their ships and sailed away. My first conflict was with a Pagan force in Kent, but when I was nineteen, my first proper battle was for your grandfather at the Battle of Farnham. I was given my own army, and when a large force of Danes landed in Kent I engaged with them at Farnham, where I caught up with them and defeated them in battle.

They fled to Benfleet in the Kingdom of Essex, where we followed and later stormed their stronghold and destroyed it. Their leader escaped to Shoebury, but as well as their longships we captured his wife and children as hostages and took them back to London.'

'What happened in the end?'

'King Alfred graciously returned his family on the condition that the Vikings leave, so they set sail from these shores and returned to where they came from.'

'What was it like, fighting the Pagans for the first time?'

'Terrifying, in all honesty. I remember we came across a Viking force lined up in front of us. Hundreds of round shields of all colours were what immediately struck me. Then the noise of the roar of the Viking men who waved their swords and spears and banged their shields. My father must have realised how frightened I was and rode up alongside me, putting his hand on my shoulder. He never said a word, just smiled then winked at me. It suddenly calmed me, but the odd thing was, for all their bravado, as soon as we charged they dispersed and ran off. But it is like anything: when you have been through an experience like that after many times, you become less anxious or afraid. It helps having men around me who would fight for you to their death. I have five thegns who are the best fighting men in all the kingdoms. They keep very close to me and strangely, however fast I ride or run, there are always at least two who keep just in front of me. They watch me closely in battle and if I seem to be struggling they are always there to turn things around. I reward them well with land and money, but nothing could repay the loyalty they show me.'

'I was only very young when my grandfather died. I remember him telling me I would be a great king one day when I grew up. Was King Alfred a great man?'

'Yes. I can tell you many stories about him. It wasn't always going his way, but he was determined to never give in to the Heathens. I was still very small and one of my earliest memories was when after Father had been defeated we were forced to hide from the Pagans at Athelney, on an ancient hill fort and almost surrounded by marsh. It was a very difficult time. I remember one evening my mother, sister and I heard men approaching and we had to put out all the candles and sit in silence in the dark because we thought it was the Pagan army coming to get us. As it turned out it was King Alfred returning with a few loyal supporters he had found.

'My sister and I used to fight each other with our wooden swords to pass the time. Which is why Athelflaed is so good with the sword. She loved to practise the military skills with the boys and could throw a spear and was a better shot with a bow than most of them, including me.

'Later I can remember my sister telling me that she had accompanied my father to Egbert's Stone, where he had asked all the Saxon ealdormen he knew in Somerset, Wiltshire and other parts of Wessex to meet up. Athelflaed said that she remembers arriving there and finding a large army of men who had come from all around to support their king. They engaged with the Danes at the Battle of Edington and my father won a decisive victory. After trapping the Danish leader, Guthrum, at Chippenham, the Danes surrendered and King Alfred, who was always chivalrous towards his enemy, accepted Guthrum as his spiritual son and he baptised the Dane, hoping he would be a loyal Christian. I am not sure Guthrum would have been quite so generous had the situation been reversed.'

'And was he? Was Guthrum as gracious to King Alfred?'

'He made a treaty with my father which divided England in half. Then he went to live in East Anglia, where he died, although that did not stop the raids from the Pagan fortune seekers. But your grandfather changed the strategy for the House of Wessex and changed the way the Saxons dealt with the Pagan invaders. He realised the importance of a navy for our kingdom, building ships to match and combat the Viking longships. He also made sure there were always fighting men available to face a crisis, even at harvest time or in winter when he was caught out before. He was very aware, however, that the army could not be everywhere and that the Saxon towns had to be able to defend themselves. So he organised the building of many burhs, the town fortifications that could repel the Vikings or keep them at bay until help arrived.'

'So he was a great leader?'

'Yes, and I intend to continue his legacy, by building more burhs, more ships and keeping the Vikings under control. But there was much more to King Alfred than just being a good military leader. He devised a code of laws for the land, with agreement from the wise council of men from whom he took advice. It gave all law-abiding people who wished to settle in England the same justice and rights, whether Saxon or Viking. He was a scholar, translating important Latin works into English. And he has been a patron of the Christian Church, building new abbeys, monasteries and churches, and promoting the Christian faith to all the people of this land. He visited Rome when he was a boy, you know. That was before the Pagans became regular visitors to our shores.'

'Heavens. We have a lot to look up to, Father.'

'Yes, a difficult act to follow. It is very important that we unite the kingdoms in England. Especially Mercia and Wessex, being the two most powerful. Which is why, although you are born a son of Wessex, you live in Mercia. Ethelred is old and is poor of health. He must be succeeded by you and your aunt, so that one day this land will become all one England.'

'Yes, I see that.'

'Asser, our Bishop of Sherborne, who was very close to my father, is still writing his biography of King Alfred. When he has finished it, when you have time, you must read it through.'

'I would like to.'

'You know, Athelstan, your grandfather had a dream once: St Cuthbert came to him in a vision and told King Alfred that he would be victorious against the Vikings and that all of Britain would be given to him and his descendants.' Edward smiled at his son and left the room, leaving Athelstan contemplating his destiny as a future king.

A few months later, as Edward sat in the great hall, the door swung open and in walked Plegmund.

'Ah, Archbishop! How was your expedition to Rome?'

'Good afternoon, My Lord. It was very, er… interesting.'

'Come and sit here and tell me all about it. What of the city itself?'

'It is a magnificent city, huge. Over half a million people with many churches and the wonderful cathedral of St Peter's where the pontiffs are buried. There is an abundance of stone buildings and of course many surviving from the Roman Empire such as the Flavian amphitheatre that they call the Colosseum. Much of it has been converted to housing and workshops.'

'Did you get your audience with Sergius?'

'Yes, although my meeting with the pontiff was rather brief. He has granted me the new bishops I required. It's just that... I am rather disillusioned, to say the least, with what is happening in Rome.'

'Really? Tell me more.'

'I spoke with a number of cardinals whilst I was there. One in particular – I can't say who, as I am sworn to secrecy – divulged that the pontiff may have gained his position by foul means.'

Edward leaned forward, curious to know more.

'It seems that he had two rivals. His predecessor, Pope Leo V, and also the man known as Christopher, the Cardinal of the Church of San Lorenzo in Rome. It is rumoured that he murdered both of them, Christopher being thrown into prison and strangled on his orders.'

'Heavens.'

'But there is more. The city is dominated and controlled by the wealthy noble family headed by Theophylact. It seems Sergius is having an affair with his teenage daughter Marozia, encouraged by her mother Theodora. What is more, not only is Marozia his mistress but she has a young son called John and the pontiff is reputedly the father. She also has other lovers, it seems.'

'Saints alive! Rome seems abound with iniquity and corruption!'

'Quite so, My Lord.'

'And do you believe all this?'

'Well, in all honesty, I don't know what to be believe. But when I was in conversation with other cardinals, they didn't seem to deny these rumours. In fact, they just shrugged their shoulders and said, "It is just the way things are in Rome right now." The events there are all rather disturbing. However, I have come back with a gift from the pontiff; he has given me some of the relics of St Blaise. Would you like me to house these here in your mother's Nunnaminster?'

'Yes, good idea. As well as building and dedicating new churches in England, I am satisfied that we continue to make every effort to convert all the Pagan people of this land to the Christian faith, but we also set an example to our priests and ecclesiastical people to live a life of sanctity and honesty. I cannot see you doing away with the churchmen you disapprove of, Archbishop! You have done a good job in reforming the Church.'

'Thank you, My Lord, and I am grateful for your support, although I think I have a little way to go. There are other wise men who must take credit. Particularly Asser. I think we will miss him when he goes.'

'I agree,' confirmed Edward.

Asser died the following year.

CHAPTER 6
THE YEAR 910
KENT

Edward was furious. He banged his fist on the table in frustration, startling the elderly Archbishop Plegmund. 'Another Pagan invasion. They land in Northumbria, led by this... so-called king, Haldane?'

'Yes, brother.' Edward relied on his brother Athelweard for counsel and to gather information for the King. 'Also Haldane's brother, we think, and another "King" called Eowils with various earls and thanes. It does raise the point, Edward, does it not, if our campaign into Northumbria last year was the right strategy. Many Pagan settlements were destroyed and their livestock taken.'

'Northumbria is often a law unto itself. It is easily reached from the Norse lands and offers easy pickings for the Pagans,' announced Plegmund.

'Yes, and our raid was revenge for the invaders rampaging Northumbria themselves. Now they have the audacity to march into Mercia on a campaign of pillage. But you may be right, brother, we need to reconsider our ideas on how we deal with the Vikings. Perhaps concentrate on consolidating our position and step up with the building of the town burhs for our Saxon people. But for now we must deal with this situation. I worry for my sister, whom I fear is being attacked on two fronts.'

'Yes, she has been building a burh at Bremesbyrig and was caught unawares, but word is that she has repelled the Viking force that sailed up the River Severn.'

'We must gather our men and march to her assistance immediately. I have had enough of these raiding forces that continually plague us. If the Pagans continue to break the peace and breach the treaty my father signed, then I will have to re-conquer the Danelaw. And most, of all, defeat these Danes in battle!'

TETTENHALL, WOLVERHAMPTON

It was a hot August evening, but darkness was fast descending. Cuthbert and Edwin, who had re-united to scout for the King, had tied up their horses and were moving stealthily through the forest towards the distant noise they could hear. At the edge of the forest they lay prone and gazed down from the trees at the top of the slope towards the little River Penk, where they could see the lights surrounding the tents of a large Danish army.

'Found them!' Cuthbert had a smug look of satisfaction as he whispered to his brother.

'Yes, I wasn't sure whether to believe that old Saxon veteran we came across yesterday when he said he had seen a foreign army down the road.'

The brothers had honed their scouting skills and were trusted and respected by the Saxon Royal family. They had roamed the surrounding countryside and had been checking the main routes back to Northumbria to where the Danish army were returning. They picked up as much information and knowledge from the local people as they could.

Cuthbert looked pensive. 'Let's return to the King and let him know. I think he will want to face them in battle as soon as possible.'

'Yes, and with Athelflaed at the head of the large Mercian army approaching fast from the west, well, surely they would be invincible.'

'I hope so, brother. We must go before we are spotted.'

They rode at some speed, reaching the King's camp a few hours later. It was late at night, but Edward was still up, with Archbishop Plegmund pacing the tent and discussing Christianity. When Cuthbert had relayed his information about the whereabouts of Halfdane and his Danish army, Edward smiled. 'They are very close to us, but what they don't realise... Athelflaed is marching down the road from Litchfield to meet me here. She must be heading almost directly for them. I know you must be tired, but I need to ask you to serve your King further this night.'

'Anything, My Lord.' Cuthbert knew he would be well rewarded for his duties to the King.

'Take fresh horses and get to Athelflaed. Tell her I am attacking the Danes tomorrow and ask for her to join me as soon as she can. She might even engage with them before we get to them. My army alone is a match for Halfdane, but if my sister can join forces, we should be far too powerful for them.'

'Is Ethelred with her?'

Edward shook his head. 'His health is very poor. He is back in Gloucester. Athelflaed leads the Mercian army these days.'

When Cuthbert and Edwin had circumnavigated Haldane's forces and reached the Mercians early next morning, they were surprised to find they were little more than two hours from where they had found the Danish army encamped.

Athelflaed was at the head of the marching army. Alongside her was her nephew, Athelstan, now sixteen and looking strong and eager. Athelflaed recognised the two approaching horsemen. 'Ah, the King's scouts. They must have news.'

'Greetings, My Lady.' Cuthbert doffed his hat and bowed his head.

Athelstan rode forward to shake the hands of the King's scouts; he knew the importance of these men. Cuthbert and Edwin felt very honoured.

'The King has sent us to let you know that about two hours along this road is the Danish army led by Halfdane that we have been searching for. They are in all probability heading this way. The King is mustering the men to advance from Wolverhampton and catch up with them.'

Athelflaed's eyes lit up. She was completely fearless. 'We have them! Excellent. We will prepare the men for battle.'

'Will you be waiting for my father before you attack?' enquired Athelstan.

olutely not! The Mercian men can take this Pagan
She winked at Athelstan, who smiled broadly.

uthbert, you and your brother may as well stay with us, but no fighting for you this day.'

'But—'

Athelstan wagged his finger at them as if to say, 'My aunt is absolutely right.'

Athelflaed asked her ealdormen and thegns to quickly gather the men around her. She addressed them from a rock on a raised section of ground.

'Men of Mercia, you will do battle today as up ahead is the Pagan army we must defeat. We have a chance to crush these Heathens, drive them from our land and give the Saxon nation a glorious victory. They have come from Northumbria and raided our Mercian villages and towns, stealing, murdering and burning. They are heading back from where they came, but we must stop them. We will soon have the help of the King, who is marching to us as we speak. So sharpen your weapons, pray to God for to assist us and prepare for a momentous day.'

The Saxon men cheered, shook their fists and waved their spears in the air. Within minutes they were back into their marching positions but quickening the pace along the ancient track.

After about two hours they came across their adversaries. Riding along the top of a ridge, the Viking army were still marching in a long line and seemed completely unaware of the Saxons. Athelflaed surveyed what was in front of her.

'We may be at a slight disadvantage in terms of numbers of men.'

'Yes, Aunt, but are they aware of Father's whereabouts?'

Athelflaed smiled a wicked smile. 'Hopefully not. In the meantime, we will attack them just as the cross that bridge.' She pointed to a footbridge over the stream, which was just slight wider than the width of a cart.

Suddenly one of the Vikings spotted the Saxon men and vanguard, hurriedly trying to form a shield wall in front of the bridge, but the first cohort of some of the best Saxon warriors advanced with archers releasing their arrows and men behind raining down their spears into the ranks of the Danes, who bellowed and roared at their opponents, trying to return their own spears. Athelstan led a party of horsemen around the left flank. The two armies clashed in hand-to-hand combat. At the centre of the action, the Saxon front line smashed their shields into the makeshift Danish wall and hacked with swords and axes at the Danes. Gaps appeared in the Danish front line and they fell back behind the bridge. The Mercian army was unable to cross the stream whilst a number of Danish thegns, with plenty of battle experience, held their side of the bridge. The riverbank was too deep to traverse. It would have been suicide to try, and so it seemed that it was stalemate at the bridge.

Meanwhile, Edward's army was marching as fast as possible towards the battlefield. Just minutes away he could hear the furore ahead.

'Come, men of Wessex,' he cried. 'Our Mercian friends have joined in battle. Let us hasten to their rescue.' The soldiers ran down the hill, giving out a massive roar. The surprised Danes looked behind to see themselves soon to be overwhelmed by the West Saxon army. Turmoil took place amongst their ranks. They were trapped between two forces. Athelflaed had stopped any possible escape route for the Danes, and Edward's horsemen rode past the Danish army to virtually surround them. Some of the Danes began to try to get across the river but were ordered back. Others tried to form a circle of shields, under the orders of their leaders. The Saxons moved in from all sides, and Edward's men ploughed in, hacking away at what was left of the shield wall. Fierce fighting continued for over an hour but gradually the Danish men began to tire. More of their number fell and eventually they tried to break out. Some managed to get to the trees and others ran the other way across the stream, but many were cut down and the others fought to the death.

Then it was all over. The carnage was terrible with bodies lying all over the field of battle. Many more Danish bodies than Saxon ones, Edwin noticed. Edward rode over to Athelflaed and embraced her then put his arm around Athelstan's shoulder. 'A great victory, sister.' The leaders were elated. The adrenalin was still running high.

'Yes.' Athelflaed had a smirk on her face. '…of course, we could have managed perfectly well on our own, but I guess you need to share the spoils of victory.'

Edward laughed out loud. 'Ha! My version of it is that we came to your rescue in the nick of time. To snatch victory from the jaws of defeat!'

'Hardly, brother. We had them on the run.' She knew he was teasing and poked him hard in the midriff.

Just then Edward's thegn Edmund appeared and bowed before the King and his sister, to whom he turned to first. 'My Lady, we have found the body of a man we believe was your foe at Chester. We think it is Ingimund the Irish Dane, identified by his shied and banner. Also, Sire, we have found the bodies of Kings Halfdane, his brother and also King Eowils. Also many earls and other notables.'

The mood changed and Edward suddenly looked solemn. He looked at Athelflaed. 'The death of a king is a serious matter, even that of an enemy king. Bring the bodies to me.'

When they carried the bloody bodies on stretchers to the King, he vowed that they would be buried with ceremony. They had stood bravely with their men and fought to the death.

'This changes the situation in our favour,' announced Edward. 'With their defeat today, the Danish influence in England has been massively weakened, particularly in Northumbria. Their main army has been decimated.'

'Yes, brother, perhaps we can rest easy for a while.'

'I wouldn't be too sure, Athelflaed. How is your husband, by the way?'

'Very sick. I don't think he has long left in this world. He has made his will and in it he wishes the boroughs of London and Oxford to you, brother.'

Ethelred died the following spring. Athelflaed became the recognised leader of all her kingdom and became known as the Lady of Mercia. It was unusual for a woman in Saxon England and proved just how much she was loved and admired by her people. Not to mention how able she was as a leader.

MALDON

A little later that year, Edwin returned back home. One autumn day, Edwin and Edgar had decided to take themselves through the Dengie peninsula to spy upon the Viking camp. Perhaps, if they were lucky, they might even be able to rescue Golderon, if she was unguarded and left alone. Edgar went to let Mildryth know of their idea.

'I am coming too.'

'No, Mildryth, it's too risky. You must stay here.'

'She is my sister and I have every right.' She gazed straight at Edgar with her big brown eyes.

'You crazy woman. So strong-willed.'

'Anyway, you will look after me.'

Edgar rolled his eyes. Edwin laughed when Edgar told him.

'That's quite a girl you have there, brother.'

'But... can't you tell her no?'

'I don't think anyone can tell Mildryth anything once she has made up her mind. She will be fine.'

The trio rode to St Lawrence Bay, named after the third-century patron saint, where they left their horses with a friend and continued on foot towards Bradwell, keeping off the main track where they could. As they approached the Viking camp, they crawled through the long grass and then into some trees just to the north. They crawled again through scrub and long grass to the edge of the camp. No sooner had they stopped than Mildryth nudged Edgar and, with her eyes, indicated a pair sitting next to a fire to their right but with their back to them. It was Golderon and Gerth. They sidled along to their right and watched the pair from a safe distance. Golderon put her head on Gerth's shoulder and Gerth put his arm around her and kissed her golden head. Edgar and Mildryth looked at each other with surprise. This was not what they were expecting at all. Suddenly, Golderon stood up and walked away to her right.

The mouths of the three onlookers dropped open. It was obvious that Golderon was heavily pregnant. As Edgar and Mildryth continued to stare at the Viking people moving about before them, Edwin poked the pair of them and beckoned them to retreat out of sight.

Once clear, they walked back along the track.

'Well!' exclaimed Mildryth. 'I didn't see that coming.'

'No. But… it seems they are genuinely happy together.'

'Something tells me that my sister has no desire to be rescued.'

'And we could leave them alone, but the problem is that we hear that these Pagans are creating problems all around the peninsular. They refuse Christianity or even to mingle with Saxon people. But worse, they still plunder the surrounding land, stealing cattle, burning farmsteads and even killing their occupants.'

'Father is reluctant to engage them in battle without more superior numbers, knowing we would suffer heavy losses.'

They continued back to where they had left their horses. There was not much more to be said concerning Golderon and the talk reverted to the harvest and problems at home.

CHAPTER 7
THE YEAR 912
MALDON

Edgar stood on the hillside above his village, holding hands with Mildryth.

'Who are they? They're coming this way, but I can't tell whether they are Saxons or Vikings.'

In the distance, led by a contingent of horsemen with flags flying and banners waving, was a great army of many men.

'Where are your brothers, Edgar?'

'Well, Cuthbert is still with the King as far as I know. Edwin is around here somewhere. He—'

'Right behind you, Edgar!' Edwin had climbed up the hill to join the inquisitive pair.

'Hello, brother. Can you make out who they are?' Edgar pointed towards the army getting ever nearer.

Edwin gazed into the distance. 'They are Saxons, I can tell. I can just make out the red banner with the Saxon white dragon, and they… Wait… I don't believe it.' He looked fervently at the man leading the army.

'What is it?'

'It's the King. See the man on the white horse! That's no less than King Edward.'

'Coming to Maldon? Are you sure?'

Edwin nodded. 'Yes, I am certain. We had better get to the village and warn Father. Make preparations.'

Half an hour later King Edward rode into the entrance to the village, where Aldwine and the Maldon thegns were waiting to welcome him. Cuthbert was amongst the King's leading followers and he embraced all his family members.

'Greetings, Edwin.' The King, dismounting his horse, smiled at his scout, who had been spending time at home with his family.

'Welcome, My Lord. This is my father, Aldwine. He is leader of the village.'

'Ah. I have heard much about you. Good to meet you.'

Aldwine bowed. 'It is an honour and a privilege, My Lord King. We were not expecting you.'

'We try to keep our movements secret so that we can catch the Danes unaware. Unfortunately we tend to surprise the Saxons too, but you need not be alarmed. The army will camp to the south. But if you can accommodate me in the village…?'

'Of course, My Lord. We will prepare a house.' He whispered in the ear of his wife and Edith scurried away. There was an empty house which she would get ready and provide with all luxuries which she could muster. It was a warm day, the first week in June, and so no fire was necessary.

'Take me to your house for now, and I will explain my plans and my proposals to you. Your family can join us.

Your sons have proved very loyal and so I am content that you whole family is trustworthy.'

'Yes, Sire.' Aldwine bowed again.

Aldwine sat with his three sons and listened attentively to their King. Edith was running around finding candles, appropriate bedding and racking her brains to think of everything a king might need.

'So, this is my intention. I would like to use your village as a base. I need to build a burgh at Witham, which Cuthbert tells me is only two hours march from here. From there I aim to take possession of all the land in Essex and beyond if possible. Anyone who will not submit to my rule will be driven from the land or taken as prisoners. I intend to return here, and on the way back from Witham I intend to improve the route to Maldon with a herepath, such as the military paths which my father built in Wessex. Maybe not this visit, but later I will help to improve the fortifications here at Maldon.'

'I see. That all makes sense. Er… Just one more thing, Sire.'

'Yes?'

'At Bradwell, not too far from here, is a Viking settlement. But they are very aggressive. In fact, they have plundered neighbouring villages, raped local women and proved to be murderous.'

'Ah yes, I believe Cuthbert warned me of this vicious and cruel band of Heathen men, so I will resolve the situation immediately. I will send my brother and two of my thegns, with some of my best fighting men and with enough of your men and their leader, we will deal with them. I cannot accept them as subjects. There is only one way to deal with such people and that is to defeat them and banish them from our lands. You know, I have come to learn that there is a wide variety of the quality and behaviour of migrating people. Some of our visitors from overseas can be friendly and wish to trade or settle with the Saxon people. But some of the Viking invaders are violent, brutal and even sadistic. Such men must be annihilated.'

The next morning the soldiers appeared from their camp armed, most with shields, some with spears, some bows and arrows, and others with swords; some with a combination of these weapons. A hundred of the armed men, which included Edgar, were ushered into three longboats that would sail down the River Blackwater to the estuary at Bradwell. Others formed into a column of men ready to march and were joined by a force from the village, including Edwin, who was now aged twenty-two and, being the son of Maldon's reeve, would lead the village contingent. King Edward would take the bulk of his army to Witham, leaving the battle with the Bradwell Pagans to his brother Athelweard, the leading thegns and Edwin.

As the King marched away with his men to Witham, Athelweard and Edwin led their armed force towards Bradwell.

Athelweard noticed that Edwin looked nervous. 'We will drive the Pagans out of this shire, Edwin. I have confidence in our army.'

'I do not have too much experience in fighting the Pagans, Sire. I prefer scouting with my brother. But this is important to me.' He explained what had happened in the battle before with the Vikings and how they had held

Golderon as hostage but that she had become part of the Viking community.

'Ah, I see the predicament. Well, either the Pagans must abide by Edward's laws and accept him as King or leave this land. And Golderon must make her choice. And I do not have too much fighting experience myself. The King would prefer I remain in Winchester, lest anything should happen to him whilst he is on campaign marauding against the Pagans. My brother is very brave, but I sometimes wonder whether he is too much so, and rather reckless at times, not preserving his own self for the good of the Saxon nation. However, today we have some excellent thegns with good fighting experience. I think we can rely on them to lead the fight against our enemy.'

After a few hours' march they began to approach their destination. Ahead the Vikings were waiting and it seemed they were in no mood to accept any Saxon interference in their community. They were lined up in battle readiness and shouted obscenities at the Saxons, goading them to attack them. Edwin was a little surprised to see some Viking warrior women amongst their ranks brandishing spears and axes. Athelweard waited and assessed the situation. When he heard that his longships were closing in from the river side, he swung the Saxon army to the south.

Just as the Saxon men disembarked from their ships to the north, Athelweard raised his arm and gave the signal to charge. The Saxons rushed forward and fiercely hacked at the Viking line. The Saxons outnumbered their foes and soon began to overwhelm them. The Vikings appeared not to have anticipated the Saxon sea force, which had set fire to Viking longships moored nearby so that they could not easily escape. They fought bravely but the outcome was inevitable. A few of the Vikings ran off but most fell fighting. Edwin was anxious to find his brother. He made his way through the melee of victorious Saxon warriors and was relieved to find Edgar standing by a group of Saxons and dead Viking men. He put his arms around his brother. Edgar pointed to Golderon, close by, kneeling over the dead body of Gerth, who had been badly hacked. Tears rolled down her cheeks.

Golderon looked up. 'He loved me, Edwin.' Standing next to her was Agnar, her little son, looking stunned and too young to really understand the consequences of what had happened.

Edwin held out his hand to her and helped her from the ground. Edgar offered to take Agnar back to Maldon in the longship but Golderon desperately wanted her son to stay with her. So Edgar found a spare horse and hoisted the little boy up onto his saddle and rode back with Edwin, who had his arm tightly wrapped around Golderon on his own horse. He did not talk to Golderon too much, for there was little he could say to comfort her at this moment. But he felt a great compassion for her.

Finally, they reached home. Mildryth, when she saw her sister, ran to her and flung her arms around her. There were tears of joy from both of them. Golderon and Agnar would share a house with her sister for the time being. But Edwin and Edgar were constant visitors over the coming weeks, making sure they were alright and helping them whenever they were needed. Golderon could see that Mildryth was madly in love with Edgar, and as the days passed she soon grew more and more fond of Edwin.

One warm, sunny day they took a walk along by the river; Agnar was throwing sticks into the water and Edwin took Golderon's hand. She looked into his eyes and they kissed tenderly.

'Would you be my wife? I will look after you. And Agnar.'

Golderon's eyes were shining bright. 'I am older than you,' she teased.

'Not by much.'

'We had better go and see your father then.'

It was all arranged. A month later the wedding day of the excited couple dawned. It had rained heavily during the night, but luckily, by the time daylight came, it was bright and warm. Mildryth and her friends fussed around Golderon, pulling her from her bed and helping her dress in her beautiful sky-blue dress and fixing a garland for her hair. After more fussing, they eventually escorted her to the Great Hall for the morning meal, where Edwin was waiting with his family in his finest tunic, in dark blue, and a gleaming gold ceremonial sword. He greeted her with a big smile and a kiss and then gave her the traditional gift of a pouch of money, with new silver pennies recently minted in the name of King Edward.

Then they all sat down at a long table to eat and drink, apple juice and big hunks of bread with cheese. There were nuts, eggs and fruit, but this would be a light meal in comparison to the big feast that was organised for after the wedding ceremony.

Golderon was sad that neither her father nor her brother were there to see her marry again and her mother had died some years before in childbirth. But her uncle was there to come to the financial arrangements with Aldwine, and of course her little sister Mildryth, who had helped out with all the wedding arrangements.

When the meal had finished, everyone gathered outside the little wooden church building. The men of the village had mounted their round shields on the wall of the church so that was a multi-coloured display as a backdrop.

Because Aldwine was a reeve and from an important family, they were very honoured to have Ceolmund, the Bishop of Rochester, who had sailed from Kent, to perform the ceremony. The two families stood close to the bride and groom whilst they made their oaths to each other. Rings were exchanged and Edwin's gold ring that he gave to his bride was crafted by his mother Edith. They were then blessed by the bishop, who finally took the couple into the church, where they knelt and prayed.

They emerged to cheers and congratulations from all around.

Later, everyone came to the Great Hall, where the long tables had been adorned with flowers and candles and heaps of food brought out for everyone to feast upon. There was roast pig, chicken, a variety of cooked birds, fish, oysters, bread and various vegetables. Also fruit and cakes with honey. To drink there was the usual mead but also some wine, brought over by the Frisian traders on the request of Edith, especially for the occasion.

The celebration continued long into the evening. Around the table Edwin sat with his new wife, Mildryth, and Edgar and soon Cuthbert joined them.

'Well, wife, I am sorry that more of your family could

not be here today, but at least you have your sister.' Edwin smiled at Mildryth.

Edgar turned to the two sisters. 'What do you think has happened to your brother Galan?'

'I dread to think,' Mildryth replied. 'He is only thirteen so hopefully they will not harm him, being so young.'

'I hate to say it, but it is common practice for the Pagans to take them away as hostages for slavery. He could be anywhere,' said Cuthbert, looking perplexed.

'Well, I will not give up on my brother,' Mildryth said.

'If I hear anything at all I will get the news to you.'

'Are you returning to scout for the King, then, Cuthbert?'

'Yes, I have another six weeks on duty before I spend time back home.'

'Any likely ladies on the horizon?' Edwin grinned at his brother.

'Maybe one of the ladies at court at Winchester. But I don't think you should be expecting a wedding for me just yet.'

'Oh well, no matter, we have Edgar's wedding to look forward to shortly. Is that right, brother?'

Mildryth suddenly looked coy. 'Next year!' she announced, looking at Edgar, who also looked bashful.

'Is that so?' Edwin ruffled Edgar's hair as Cuthbert and Golderon applauded.

At that moment Aldwine came over to see his three sons. 'Come and dance. There is too much serious talk going on here and not enough making merry and celebrating.'

CHAPTER 8
THE YEAR 914
WINCHESTER

Between forays, the King had found time to spend back in his beloved Winchester. In his palace that October, he was enjoying life with his family. Athelstan was in discussion with his stepmother, Aelfflaed, about St Cuthbert and they were considering what items they could donate to his tomb. The King was trying to have a conversation with the Bishop of Winchester, but his two young sons Alfweard and Edwin were romping around their feet and making such a racket that the King was having difficulty being heard.

'Boys, quieten down. Give me some peace.'

'Yes, Father.' And Alfweard picked up a wooden sword and chased his brother across the room.

Edward chuckled. It was nearly time for their education to take place, but in the meantime he would let them have their fun. He looked over at two of his daughters, who were playing with their rag dolls.

'It is good to be back in Wessex, Bishop. I really should spend more time with my family.'

'Yes, My Lord. It would be very agreeable if you could spend most of your time here, but sadly the Heathen raiders constantly distract you.'

The King nodded. But just as he was thinking that perhaps there might be a period of peace and calm, he was interrupted by Cuthbert, who entered the Great Hall escorted by his brother Edwin and was there to shatter his illusions.

'My Lord, we have had news that I fear will not please you. A fleet of Viking ships has sailed up the River Severn and are rampaging through the land in Wales and now in Mercia. It is the Danish earls Ohter and Harald with a sizeable force, though we do not know exactly how many.'

'Where is Athelflaed? Can she confront them?'

'The last we heard, Sire, is that she was at Mersey, where she had taken command of the communities there and was fortifying it.'

'Oh yes, of course, I had forgotten.'

'Her exact whereabouts now are uncertain, but she is still in that region. I will send out parties to find her.'

The King sighed and folded his arms. 'And I was intending to secure Buckingham with two Saxon burghs on either side of the River Ouse. Then we were due to meet up. But Buckingham will have to wait.'

'Er… there is another problem, My Lord. Ohter has taken Bishop Cyfeiliog as a hostage. We think he has been taken back to the Viking ships.'

'Oh, wonderful,' the King groaned sarcastically. 'He is a very noble and worthy man who has done much good work in spreading the Christian message and converting the local people at Archenfield and the area of the borderlands between Wales and Mercia. We need to get him back by foul means or fair. Well then…' he turned to the Bishop of Winchester, 'we had better mobilise our men. Send out the message to all those on duty for this half year and tell them to arm themselves and gather here within two days.' He glanced at his wife. She looked glum and crestfallen.

'I know. You have to leave, and I suppose I only have a few days with you.'

'Actually, I will be leaving with an advance guard first thing tomorrow. Sorry, my love, but I fear Bishop Cyfeiliog's life hangs in the balance. I need to get to the scene of the problem as soon as I can. My brother can look after everyone here.'

'Hmm… such is the life of a wife of a king.'

'You and your brother get a good night's rest, Cuthbert. I will be needing you tomorrow.'

Cuthbert was quite excited about the prospect.

CHIPPENHAM

With a few hundred men on horseback, the King set out heading westwards. It was a dangerous venture as he would be in danger if he encountered the whole Viking force. On the fourth day, he reached the town of Chippenham. Entering through the walls of the city, he was welcomed by the townspeople, who had been notified of the King's approach by Cuthbert and his patrols. The ealdermen greeted the King and escorted him to the abbey quarter, where the King would be housed next to the abbey. On the way, Edward looked at the walls re-built by his father, who had re-organised the town and supplied men to defend it. Two young teenage boys gazed down in awe at their King, who, after the Battle of Tetenhall, now had a fearsome reputation that had spread throughout England.

Recently the King had authorised a mint for the town.

'I wish to visit the mint ealdorman. I will need £50 of silver coin.'

'Goodness, that is a lot of money. I will arrange for the supervisor to meet with you and provide you with the coin reserve.'

The King nodded. 'I have good use for it.'

The next day Cuthbert was sent out with his scouts to find the Heathen army and report back. He rode with Edwin and two other men together, but after an hour heading west at a junction of tracks the group split into two pairs, with Cuthbert and Edwin heading on a more northerly route. They all agreed to meet back in Chippenham in three days' time. The next day Cuthbert and Edwin rode through forests and fields, reaching a high point where in the distance he could see the great River Severn to the west. They descended down into a valley with a little stream, bordered on both sides with trees. As they ambled to the bottom, they were suddenly confronted by six Viking horsemen who appeared out of the trees. Another four mounted men seemed to appear from nowhere to approach them from behind. There was little doubt that these were the Viking leader's own scouts, and in a moment, somewhat surrounded, Cuthbert had to think very quickly. He stopped and held up his hand in a gesture that suggested he wanted to talk.

'We come in peace with a message from King Edward, leader of the Saxon nation.' He spoke loudly, trying to sound confident but fearing they might be attacked by this small force of intimidating-looking men. Edwin looked terrified.

One of the Vikings looked directly at him and spoke. 'Where is your King?'

Cuthbert saw no reason to lie at this stage and so replied, 'He is with his army at Chippenham, a day's ride. He would like to talk with Earl Ohter.'

'For what reason?'

'The King has not confided in me as to the nature of such talks, but he has instructed me to find Earl Ohter and arrange a meeting between the two of them.'

The spokesman for the Viking scouts hesitated. 'Follow us.' And the men turned and continued down to the end of the valley, with Cuthbert and Edwin being escorted with the Vikings in front and behind. After a surprisingly short ride, they arrived at the Viking camp, where blank, staring faces stood and watched them as they made their way to a large tent in the middle of the camp. They were led into where a rather overweight bearded man sat drinking and playing a board game with another man who turned out to be Earl Harald. The scout introduced everyone and then spoke to his lord in his native tongue as it seemed that Ohter struggled with the Saxon tongue.

'The earl wishes to know what your King would like to talk about and what he would gain from such a meeting.'

'Er, well, King Edward would like to welcome Earl Ohter to this land and would wish to know his intentions.' Cuthbert was making this up as he went along.

Another conversation took place between the Viking scout and his earl. 'His intention is to defeat your King in battle. But he wishes to occupy this land in the meantime.'

'I am sure King Edward would consider your settlement here. He would still like to meet with your earls.'

Earl Harald scoffed and suddenly spoke in English. 'Huh, I doubt if he would agree to us being here at all!'

Ohter spoke to his scout, who turned to Cuthbert with a deadpan look on his face. 'The earl says he could cut off your heads and send them back to Chippenham in a sack.'

Cuthbert felt his heart thumping and his temperature rise. Sweat appeared on his forehead. He tried to keep his cool. 'This would very much vex our King and his sister, the Lady of Mercia, who is returning with her army to her palace near here at Gloucester.' It was about time, thought Cuthbert, that he would try to call the Heathen's bluff.

A further conversation between Ohter and Harald took place which began to get rather heated. But Ohter, it seemed, had the last word. He spoke to Harald, who exclaimed, 'Go and tell your King that he will meet him outside the town of Chippenham in two days and will barter with him. I presume he wishes for the return of the bishop, which we will consider if the terms and conditions are favourable.'

Cuthbert blew a puff of relief. As he and Edwin went to leave, Harald leapt up and grabbed Edwin by the arm. 'Not him. He can stay as our hostage.'

Edwin looked scared and Cuthbert, perplexed, nodded to his brother. 'Don't worry, Edwin, I will speak to the King.'

The Viking scout saw Cuthbert to his horse and watched him as he rode away.

Two big Danish warriors marched Edwin to the far side of the camp. He was shoved with some force into a stout wooden cage and they hauled him by a rope up into the branch of a large oak tree, where the cage dangled and swayed in the wind. It was not big enough to stand in nor to stretch his legs out. A half-filled flagon of water was the only other item in the cage, and Edwin, desperately thirsty, began to gulp down the lukewarm water.

'Don't drink it all at once. You will not get any more until tomorrow.'

Edwin was aware that the voice came from above and suddenly realised that just above him was a second cage on a slightly higher branch.

'I am Bishop Cyfeiliog. And who may you be, young man?'

Edwin, by pressing his face to the cage, could just make out a gaunt and troubled-looking man with a long beard. 'Oh, Bishop. I am Edwin and I have been escorting my brother, Cuthbert, one of King Edward's scouts. We were ambushed by the Viking scouts.'

'Well, it is good to have someone to talk to.' The bishop gazed down at the ground below, where a Viking guard was sat against a tree but seemed disinterested in the conversation happening above him. 'Where is your brother now?'

'He is returning to the King, who is aware of your plight and hopes to negotiate your release. I am here as hostage in the meantime.'

Some of the anxiety that showed on the bishop's face disappeared. 'Well, that's good to know. I didn't realise that the King himself would get involved. Perhaps there is hope for us yet.'

'How long have you been here, Bishop?'

'Three days. Not too long, but I have had to live on water and flatbread, and not too much of that either. Try to stretch your legs as often and as much as possible, or you will suffer cramps and leg pains.' The bishop paused. 'What are our chances, I wonder?'

'My brother will do everything he can to rescue us, I know.'

'Well, I hope he is able to reach the King and return to rescue us. Otherwise I fear we will suffer torture and death at the hands of these Pagans. We had better pray, my son.'

Cuthbert rode as fast as his horse could cope back to Chippenham. The next day he arrived at the town and immediately asked to urgently see his King, who could see from his scout's face that all was not well.

'What ails you, Cuthbert?'

Cuthbert explained all the recent events. 'I am so sorry, My Lord. I took your name in vain, but… I did not know what else to say. I feared the Heathens would kill me. And they have my brother as hostage.'

Edward smiled. 'Have no fear, Cuthbert. You did very well. And it so happens I do wish to bargain with this despicable Ohter, though it pains me to do so. And we will get Edwin back. I believe Lady Athelflaed is hurrying back to Gloucester and tomorrow I would like you to return there, wait for her arrival and give your report to her. I intend eventually to crush this force.'

'Yes, of course, My Lord.' The next day Cuthbert set out for Gloucester.

The King, meanwhile, waited for Ohter, who duly

turned up with his brother and thirty horsemen. In the rear was a cart holding the hostages the bishop and Edwin. Ohter stopped short of the town walls and remained there until Edward rode out with a number of his own cavalry which matched Ohter's number. The men faced each other on their horses in the open field, either side of a little brook.

Edward spoke first. 'Unless you wish to settle here in peace you are not welcome. What are your intentions?'

Ohter's brother spoke in a surly manner for the Vikings. 'We have come to see what this land can offer us.'

'But rampaging and burning the countryside and abducting our people. This does not go down to well with us.'

'It is just a matter of survival, King.'

'I am prepared to offer you a ransom for the return of the hostages and only on the condition that you leave. £20 of silver.'

The two brothers had a brief conversation. 'You will have to do better than that. We were expecting at least double.'

Edward hesitated. '£40 then. That is a great deal of money. And then you will leave and return to your country?'

Ohter smiled a devious smile and nodded. Edward beckoned to his men to bring up the cart with the chest of money. The bishop and Edwin were released and gratefully scrambled across the brook, where they were helped by Edmund, the big Saxon thegn, assisting them back to the same cart where the money had been kept. Ohter opened the lid of the chest and checked its contents of silver coin. Once satisfied, he signalled to leave. Edward had no faith in their promise to leave but at least he had the hostages. If they failed to return to their longboats he would harass and chase them until they either left or were defeated.

GLOUCESTER (GLEAWECEASTRE)

After staying overnight at Stroud, Cuthbert entered the city of Gloucester the following day. The town had been well fortified over the last decade by Athelflaed and her husband. They had added more streets and established a mint under the authorisation of Edward. It was bustling with plenty of market activity. There was the typical Saxon street plan within the burgh. Cuthbert made his way to the north of the town, where the Royal house of Kingsholm next to St Oswald's Priory was to be found.

He reported to the guards, showing his badge containing the King's seal. 'I have to report important news to our Lady Athelflaed.'

The guards looked doubtful and trusted nobody. The security was tight here. 'Our Lady of Mercia is not here.'

'Yes, I was told I may need to wait for her arrival from Mersey.'

The two guards looked at one another. This scout was certainly well informed. 'You cannot stay here. Lord Athelstan wants privacy and quiet.'

'Athel... Lord Athelstan is here?'

'Yes, just returned from Warwick.'

'It is imperative I see him.'

One of the guards sighed. 'Wait here. I will ask if he will see you.'

After a few minutes the guard returned. 'Come this way.' He led Cuthbert into a great hall. Athelstan was writing at a table. Cuthbert wished that he could read and write much better than his rudimentary skills allowed.

'My Lord, this is the man—'

'Ah, Cuthbert!' Athelstan interrupted. 'Good to see you again. Is there any truth of the rumours of a Pagan force running riot around us?'

'Yes, exactly so, My Lord.' He explained that the King was waiting to meet Ohter, who was holding hostages, but that ultimately a battle was likely to ensue when the conditions were right.

'Mmm… Lady Athelflaed is some distance away still. She has been very tired lately; in fact, she has not been well. She will need to rest. I can get the Mercian men ready in two days and march south, if you will accompany me.'

Over the next couple of days the men at Gloucester were mustered and carts loaded with food supplies and weapons. Athelstan took silver coin from the Gloucester Mint to pay his men and a few Welsh and loyal Danish mercenaries who had been baptised into Christianity. Early in the morning they set out, heading westwards, with Cuthbert scouting in front to try to spot the invading Heathens. As he travelled across a high plateau, he saw smoke billowing up into the air a few miles at most to the south. Then he realised there were a number of smoke columns. This was a giveaway, conducive to the burning of a village. He immediately returned to Athelstan's marching columns to report what he had seen.

'That will be them then.' He turned to his thegns. 'We will increase our pace.' The army steered to their right to march directly towards the smoke and came across the village in question, where they were met with a dreadful scene of devastation. It was a little community of seven houses and a communal hall in the middle. All the buildings except one were in various stages of burning. A few of them were virtually burnt out, with ashes still smouldering. Some were still burning and the hall was still in flames, which licked around the roof. The cracking of the timbers could be heard and one end had started to collapse. Nearby lay the bloody bodies of four men, one with a spear protruding from his back. There was no sign of the village livestock. There was one house left which looked charred but seemingly the fire had been extinguished or had not taken hold. At the door were the surviving women and children, huddled together. As Athelstan approached, one of the distraught women could see he was a man of nobility and threw her arms out in despair, tearfully appealing to him.

'Why...? Why us? There was no reason for them to do this to us?'

Athelstan looked down from his horse at the pitiful sight before him. 'I am sorry for this. These Viking invaders are a ferocious force of Heathens who care for nothing and no-one. I will leave some of my men to help you rebuild your village, but I need to pursue these evil men.' He asked which way they went and one of the young boys pointed to the road leading westwards. He felt anger and a determination to destroy the murderous Vikings, although he was aware that there were occasions when Saxon warriors had in the past been equally cruel to Danish communities, especially in Northumbria.

He was anxious to catch up with them and left the burning village immediately. Within less than an hour they came face to face with their adversaries.

'Looks like the Pagan scouts have seen us coming too.' The Danes were lined up in formation with a wall shield. Knowing that it could not have been King Edward who must have been some distance behind them, they had decided to make a stand. What they had not realised is that Athelstan, knowing he had superior numbers, had left his Hereford men a little way behind, concealed by the landscape. These Hereford men, who were led by some formidable thegns, would wait until the two opposing forces clashed in combat.

Athelstan's Gloucester men rushed in formation towards the Viking front line who stood shield to shield. During the melee that ensued, the Hereford men along with the Welsh were given the signal and they ran onto the battlefield, outflanking the Vikings on both sides. A terrible slaughter took place. The Heathen army fought bravely but were in total disarray and suffered great losses. Whilst some of his men gave chase to the surviving Vikings who had fled, Athelstan rode through the battlefield. Some of his men signalled to him to view some bodies they had found.

'My Lord, these two dead bodies lying here are Earl Harald and Ohter's brother. There is no sign of Earl Ohter.'

'I see. He has either escaped or he is with another force elsewhere. We will continue south to meet with my father.'

Two captured Vikings were then brought forward by Saxon thegns requesting to speak to Prince Athelstan, who demanded to know, 'Where is Earl Ohter?'

One of the Viking men stepped forward and knelt before the Saxon leader. 'My Lord, he has stayed with the longships on the big river.' He pointed westwards towards the River Severn.

'What are his intentions? Where will he go?'

'I know not, My Lord. I would happily tell you if I knew. He has several hundred men with him, but he does not wish to return home. Would you allow us, My Lord, to take away our earl so that we can give him a proper Viking funeral?'

Athelstan paused. He nodded and gesticulated for the Pagans to take away Harald's body.

A cart drew up loaded with spades and shovels. The remaining Vikings were ordered to dig a large pit in which to bury the bodies of all the dead men on the battlefield from both sides.

As twilight descended, the body of Earl Harald and Earl Ohter's brother were laid on the back of a cart and transported down to the coast.

By the time they reached the River Severn a large fire beacon guided them to where a single longship was moored. Tinder and wood had been loaded onto the front of the boat. The bodies were laid in the back with their shields laying on top of them. Two Viking warriors lit the tinder and several more pushed the boat out into the water. Athelstan suddenly realised that there were several Viking longships anchored some distance away out into the mighty river, watching the events from afar. As the burial boat drifted out over the water the flames spread to the sail and within moments the ship was a fireball. As the flames died down and the hulk burned, the ship began to sink. Eventually, there was nothing but the reflection of a golden moonlight across the water.

Two days later, from his camp on the River Severn estuary, Athelstan rode south to Chippenham with a small entourage including Cuthbert, having sent his army back home. As they approached the town, about half a mile away, they came across Edward, who was just leaving with a large force of men. As the two came towards each other there were big smiles on both their faces. They grasped each other's hand. Cuthbert was greatly relieved to see his brother not far behind the King and rushed to greet him. Athelstan reported to his father about defeat of the Pagans and the death of Earl Harald.

'Once again you have done well, my son.'

'Thank you, Father, but where are you heading?'

'This morning we received a visit from a father and his son who had come from the village of Watchet on the north Wessex coast. It seems Ohter, despite his promise to leave, is now causing much grief in that part of Wessex. His last known location is east of there and we are on the way to deal with him once and for all.'

'He watched the cremation of Earl Harald yesterday from a safe point out in the river. He must have sailed from there yesterday. Unfortunately, Athelflaed's fleet is up north where she has been having burhs built.'

'Yes, it is difficult to co-ordinate our fleet and the army at short notice. I have ships in the east of the kingdom, at the estuary of the River Thames. You look tired, Athelstan.'

'Yes, it has been a gruelling few days.'

'Go into town and rest. I will tackle Ohter. He has lost many men and is no match for my Wessex men, either in ability or number.'

'I think I will. Then probably return to Gloucester to and wait for Aunt Athelflaed. As you know, we have more plans for sweeping deeper into the Danelaw and taking control of that land and their people.'

'Excellent. Farewell and take care.'

The next day Edward set out for Watchet with his whole army, along with some of Athelstan's Gloucester men who had decided to assist the King in his fight against Ohter and his Vikings. They moved swiftly along the north Somerset coast, coming eventually to the village of Watchet. The local people told the King that they had seen Vikings scouting the area, and on hearing about the approaching Saxon army, the Pagan army was moving away westward. The King continued westward but left a large contingent of his men at Watchet to protect the village. Cuthbert went ahead and located the Viking camp near Minehead. But by this time darkness was descending and so the King was forced to make camp to the south, but he stationed lookouts along the coast and to the south in the countryside in an attempt to surround his enemy.

The next morning, at daybreak, the King rose and dressed himself, putting on his chain shirt and his helmet, and arming himself with his favourite sword. He left his tent and rode to a ridge to view the Viking camp, only to find, to his dismay, that they had disappeared in their longboats during the night. Not knowing exactly which way they went, he sent scouts out both east and west. Frustrated, he sat outside his tent in the late September sunshine and waited for news. It was early afternoon and Edward was dozing in his chair when Cuthbert, who had been sent east, rode back into camp. One of his thegns did not recognise him and drew his sword.

'Keep calm. It is my chief scout.'

Cuthbert dismounted. 'My Lord, the Pagans tried to land at Watchet in the night, not realising that our fyrd was there. They were pushed back to the beach, where they tried to re-board their boats. They were chased off with a number of losses or captured men. Our losses were virtually nil.'

The King nodded with satisfaction. 'Good. Which way were they heading?'

'They were sailing west, heading back towards this way.'

'Have a rest and some sustenance, Cuthbert. Then I will need you to go out again to see if you can find them. You have a knack of discovering their whereabouts.'

'Thank you, My Lord.' Cuthbert bowed and retreated to his tent, where he lay down. Before long his eyes grew heavy and he fell into a slumber.

An hour later he awoke, and as he walked out, he saw a man who was running into the camp and trying to gain the attention of Edmund, one of the thegns.

'My village has been raided by a Viking force,' Cuthbert heard him say.

He ran over. 'Where is your village?'

'Porlock, Sire, to the west.'

'Come with me. I am the King's scout, I will take you to him.' He looked to Edmund, who acknowledged Cuthbert and signalled his approval.

The Saxons left a number of men to guard the camp and immediately set out for Porlock, just six miles away. As they got nearer, Edward ordered his thegns to take their men both left and right, once more in an attempt to surround the

Vikings, who were caught by surprise and immediately fled towards where they had left their longships. The stragglers were cut down and a contingent of men intercepted them as they got to the beach. The Viking ships had begun to set sail and dozens of Viking men ran into the sea and started to swim towards their ships. They were hauled aboard by the occupants and just about two hundred and fifty men had survived to sail away, crammed into just four of their snekkja boats, the smaller longship so common to Norwegian Vikings. There were more than sixty men in boats that normally held forty.

The Saxons waded into the sea, firing burning arrows at the boats. Most were successfully put out, but some caught the sails, which started to alight on two of the ships. The Vikings were forced to row and headed up the River Severn.

Edward rode onto the beach on his white stallion. He looked out to sea and watched the Viking longships as they sailed further away. He turned to Edmund, his Chief thegn. 'We will not pursue these Heathens any further. The majority of their army has been decimated. I will leave some of my horsemen with you and Cuthbert to follow them along the shoreline just to try and monitor their movements. In the meantime I will return to Winchester.'

It was three weeks later that Cuthbert returned to Winchester to make his report to the King. As he entered the palace he was told that the King was not there but was hunting in the Royal forest which was north of the road from whence Cuthbert had come. He was given instructions as to how to get to the King's hunting lodge, where it was likely that he could be found.

So Cuthbert made his way back along the highway and then north onto the main track that ran through the forest. At last he came to a clearing where the King's grand hunting lodge stood. There was no-one there, but Cuthbert could hear the distant sound of dogs, and he guessed it was the hounds that accompanied the Royal hunting retinue. The barking became louder and so he waited a while, and sure enough, minutes later the hunting party appeared. Cuthbert knew that hunting was a popular pastime of the Saxon royalty. Although it was a leisure activity for the King rather than for essential food, as was the case back home, it was also important for training and exercising the horses and the dogs, and practising the skills that would be required on the battlefield. If the opportunity presented itself they would spend their leisure time with friends and other nobility and the entourage that was required to hunt in the Royal forests. Wolves, boars and deer were amongst the animals that could be found.

The party appeared into the clearing by the lodge with a large boar being carried on a pole by the King's servants. One of the riders brought to the attention of the King the presence of Cuthbert, who dismounted and bowed before Edward.

'Ah, so what became of that Heathen rabble, then, Cuthbert?'

'Well, My Lord, after you departed, we managed to track them along the shore of the great River Severn. They disembarked at Steepholme Island in the Channel, some six miles offshore, where they stayed for the night. Thegn Edmund himself led a raid in the night by taking a small sailboat on a dangerous venture out into the Channel with just a few men. He successfully set fire to three of the longships. The surviving one left next day, presumably to send for help, leaving most of the Pagans on the island. There they stayed for over a week. When we visited the island afterwards, we found that many must have died of starvation, for Steepholme is a barren place and there is no food. We sent a small sailing vessel to keep an eye on them. Eventually, two longboats turned up to look for any survivors and they sailed away down the river. Bishop Cyfeiliog, who appreciates what you did for him, incidentally, has evidently been interested in the outcome, and he sent a message to let us know that they had briefly landed on the coast in the Welsh kingdom of Dyfed. They left two days later heading west towards Ireland.'

'Good riddance to them. Do we know if Ohter was with them?'

Cuthbert could only shrug his shoulders. 'Sorry, My Lord, but we have no way of knowing.'

'And where is Edmund now?'

'I rode ahead. He is on the way, My Lord, and should be back in Winchester in a few hours.'

'Then I will wait for him. He will be well-rewarded, but I will need him to come with me into Mercia tomorrow. Whilst Athelflaed is still in the north I will be taking over the town Buckingham and intend to restore and improve the burh that my father had built there previously, build a second burh on the other side of the River Ouse and man them both with Saxons to protect the town.'

BUCKINGHAM

Within a week Edward was travelling to Buckingham to take command of the town and then supervise the works on the burhs. He was fully expecting some opposition from the Viking population there and so had sent Cuthbert on ahead to explore the outskirts and the approach road to Buckingham. Cuthbert rode along for some distance until he realised that he was just a few minutes' ride from the town and had seen virtually nobody. He very cautiously rode up to the entrance, where a single Viking was standing. He could see that Cuthbert was a Saxon of some eminence.

'Is King Edward coming here?'

Cuthbert was aghast at how this man would know such a thing. 'Yes, how did you know this?'

'Well, Earl Thurcytel, who is the Viking leader here, has been in communication with the Lady of Mercia and she has told him that the King wishes to take command and protect the Danes that live here.'

That's one way of putting it, thought Cuthbert.

'I am one of the King's scouts. He will be here shortly.'

'Oh, greetings. I am one of the earl's scouts. Along with the earls from Bedford and Northampton, he wishes to meet with your master upon his arrival, to do homage and welcome him to the town.'

'I see. In that case I will go back and inform the King.'

On the way to returning to Edward's marching men, Cuthbert got to thinking that the reputation of King Edward was spreading throughout Mercia and he guessed that they considered that it was better for the Vikings to submit to him rather than oppose him. He reported back to Edward, who smiled with satisfaction on hearing this news. The welcoming committee was there waiting by the mill.

A distinguished man with a grey beard stepped forward. 'Lord, I am Earl Thurcytel.' The other earls of Bedford and Northampton introduced themselves.

'And the earl from Cambridge? Is he here?'

'Er, he is indisposed, Sire, but he has instructed us to represent him and talk on his behalf. I think I can speak for all of us when I say that we would like to welcome you here and recognise you as the true King of this land, as we have heard that you are just and fair. Are you happy for my people to stay here and for me to govern the town?'

'Well, that depends, Earl. If the Danes remain peaceful and are willing to accept Saxons. You would be answerable to me or my designated representative. And would the Danes accept baptism into the Christian faith? As I intend to have a new church built here.'

'Sire, we already have many Saxons living here in harmony with us. They, and some of the Danish citizens, have already adopted the Christian faith. I would be content to work alongside a Saxon ealdorman or thegn.'

Earl Thurcytel seemed to be agreeing to all the King's terms and conditions. 'I will be improving the defences here and building a new burh on the other side of the River Ouse. Both will need the manpower of the townsmen, whatever their nation, and more Saxon men will be assigned to safeguard these fortifications.'

The earl bowed to the King, still mounted on his horse.

'Work will start tomorrow. I intend to stay here for three or four weeks until it is complete.' The King looked directly at the Viking earl who came from Bedford. 'And similar works will be carried out next year at Bedford.' The other earls bowed and Earl Thurcytel, after declaring his oath of allegiance and giving gifts to Edward, arranged a feast for later and showed the King to his quarters.

CHAPTER 9
THE YEAR 916
MALDON (MAELDUN)

In midsummer, King Edward had returned to Maldon. He sat in the hall which was located in the centre of the village and served as the meeting place for the townsfolk, who had gathered to hear him speak,

'I need to re-fortify the burh of this village. Deepen the ditch and extend it further, enlarging the village so that you can provide a proper marketplace and you will have room to build more houses. Repair the streets, but obviously the mill and the church will remain untouched. The palisade fencing will also be heightened. If there is time I will construct a wall on the north side of the town along by the riverside. Viking longships can invade the village from the river if they cannot break the defences elsewhere. I will provide a north gate to the river. We can keep the present jetty but add a larger one to accommodate more traders and the Frisian and Frankish merchants from over the sea. All this work will need much manpower. All the men of the village above twelve years old will need to help. I will provide many men of the army and there are forty Danes whom I have captured who will also be put to work.'

Aldwine knew these were virtually slaves who were held by the King.

'And when the work has finished, I would like you to accept the Danes into your village if they wish to stay. They would like to settle here in England.' Aldwine looked horrified. Edward smiled.

'I have family hostages and any problems they cause will result in the penalty of death. But they can be a credit to your community. Amongst them, there are boat builders, weapon makers, fishermen, potters and more.'

'I understand, Sire.' Aldwine looked at Edwin and shrugged.

'And now for rest. Tomorrow we will start work.'

Early the next morning the village community and Edward's army were a hive of activity. Some of the soldiers appeared from their camp carrying spades and wheeling barrows.

The men were marshalled into groups around the perimeter of the village wall, some digging on the east side of the village and others on the west side. The ditch became ever deeper as the earth at the bottom was removed and spread around the upper edges of the ditch. The east and west diggers worked inwards towards the middle. Edward strolled around giving instructions here and advice there. When he was satisfied with the increased depth of the ditch, his carpenters rolled out the wood for the palisade which was a stout fence completely surrounding the inside of the ditch. In the middle was a solid wooden bridge crossing the ditch. Two smaller bridges were built on the east and west sides. High gates were installed at all three bridges.

The next day two lookout towers were constructed on the east and west sides and a wooden walkway built along the south side. A short sloping revetment was added and a wooden wall with a gate was installed on the northern riverside and a new jetty was built into the River Blackwater. A high beacon was assembled and raised near to the hall which could be set alight to warn the surrounding countryside of impending attack.

When it was all finished Edward took Aldwine around the new burh to inspect the defences.

'What do you think, Aldwine?'

'Excellent, My Lord. A huge improvement and the people of the village now have a greater sense of security. We are very grateful.'

At that moment, one of the King's messengers appeared from Winchester. 'Sire, a delegation came to Winchester two days ago from Buckingham. The Bishop of Worcester and a representative from Earl Thurcytel.'

'Oh yes.'

'The earl is leaving Buckingham for the land of the Franks overseas and taking with him many of his followers.'

Edward rolled his eyes and tutted. 'Yes, I was aware that since I had designated the bishop and one of our thegns to assist in the running of the town, there has been some friction between them and the earl. They couldn't seem to agree on anything.'

'The earl says that you would supply the earl with boats on the east coast.'

'Did I say that? Mmm, well, I will give him five longboats.

If he needs more he must provide them for himself. I will make them available from here at Maldon and he can go with my blessing. Tell the bishop he may assign the Thegn or whoever he likes to govern Buckingham.'

'Yes, My Lord.' The messenger left to return to Winchester.

A few days later two hundred Vikings with Earl Thurcytel rolled into Maldon. The earl looked sombre, Edwin thought. There was no request to speak to the King and the men loaded up the boats and within a short while were sailing up the Blackwater estuary and out into the open sea.

CHAPTER 10
THE YEAR 917
COLCHESTER (COLNECEASTRE)

Edward's army had made their way from Maldon, briefly calling at Witham for sustenance, and as darkness fell, they stopped at a field a few miles south of the old Roman town of Colchester. This had become a Saxon town after the departure of the Romans, but it had been controlled and settled by the Danes for the last forty years or so. Cuthbert and a small band of his scouting party were acting as lookout on raised ground above their camp. Cuthbert reported to the King a few hours later.

'Nothing to report so far, My Lord.'

'I am hoping that the assault on the town will be a surprise attack. I intend to liberate this town and avenge the murder of St Edmund by the Heathen Ivar, who ruled here in my father's time and cut off Edmund's head just because he would not renounce Christ.'

'It was told that he was whipped and beaten before.'

'From what I hear, the current leader is not much better, cruel and vindictive.'

'Yes, My Lord. I have heard that the Saxon people have been suffering in this region. I will return to my scouting party and report to you of any changes or Pagan movement.'

'I am grateful, Cuthbert.'

Before daybreak the next day, everyone was woken. Edward gave instructions to his thegns that their men must carry no torches. The men should, however, carry ladders, one between two men, as Colchester was still defended by the old Roman walls for the most part. There was to be complete silence on the short march to the town and the carts to be left a good distance behind. No horses, as everyone, including the King, would proceed on foot. In the vanguard was the King, with his personal bodyguard, and Cuthbert, who was to keep the army on a narrow path that ran almost parallel with the main track into town.

They stealthily advanced closer and closer. There was a hint of a sunrise, but it was still quite dark and gloomy with grey clouds. As they neared the gates of the city, the King, with arm signals, sent some men towards the west gate and a smaller band of men to the south gate. At the west gate the King brought forward two of his best archers. At his order, from some distance they let fly towards the Viking guards at the gates. One dropped immediately, but the other received only an arm wound and he shouted to the men in the town, most still sleeping.

With a loud shout the Saxon army charged into the town. Many were already at the gate and the few Viking armed men that tried to stop them were overpowered. Dozens of ladders scaled the walls on two sides of the town. The Saxons poured into the town in great numbers. Most of the Viking men tried to escape over the east wall. Some were cut down as they tried to scale the wall and others threw down their weapons, indicating that they wished to surrender. Others managed to escape into the Essex countryside, disappearing into the woods. The women came out of their houses and huddled their children close to them. A small contingent of Viking warriors held out by the tower in the corner of the town and fought to the bitter end, but within a few hours it was all over. The Vikings were at the mercy of the King, who strode into the centre of the town with his thegns, at the intersection of the old Roman streets. King Edward's groom brought up his white horse, which the King mounted so that he could be seen by everyone.

'Listen to me, Viking people of Colchester, your men have been defeated and your vile leaders that were captured have been executed. This town will be governed by a Saxon ealderman and his thegns. The women and children that remain will be allowed to leave in their boats or live outside the town walls. If you agree to live in peace then you may be allowed to return to the town under the will and judgement of the ealderman.'

Some of the remaining Viking men, mostly the teenagers or the older men, were led away, and Cuthbert knew these would be subject to becoming slaves or, if they were lucky, exchanged for Saxon slaves or prisoners. Saxon horsemen were sent out into the countryside to seek out any surviving Heathen warriors and to subjugate the surrounding Danish farmers, who must agree

Over the course of the day, things settled down in the town and the Saxon soldiers temporarily moved into the houses previously occupied by the Viking families. Edward started to make plans for the re-fortification of Colchester, but in the meantime guards were posted at the gates of the outer wall and lookouts on top of the walls. In late afternoon one of the men on the wall spotted a poor, bedraggled man staggering his way along the road into the town. Looking tired, he slowly made his way to the entrance, where he was challenged by the guards.

'Who are you?'

'I have travelled from far away. But I used to live with my family at Bradwell and I was born at Maldon. I was told by a traveller that the King himself has freed this town. My name is Galan.'

'The two guards looked at each other. 'Cuthbert comes from Maldon, doesn't he?'

'Cuthbert? I think he may know me.'

'I will go and find him.'

Galan was led inside the town and he sat down, exhausted. After ten minutes the guard reappeared with Cuthbert, who looked at the dishevelled individual.

'You are Galan?' The man nodded. 'I knew a Galan once in Maldon. He had a sister.' Cuthbert was inviting Galan to identify himself.

'I have two sisters, Golderon and Mildryth.'

Cuthbert gave Galan a broad grin. 'Well, well. That makes us kin, then, Galan. Your sister Golderon is married to my brother Edwin.' He shook Galan's hand.

'Heavens. That's a surprise. It is a relief to come across a friendly face, Cuthbert. Can we journey back to Maldon tomorrow? It will be good to get back to familiar surroundings.'

Cuthbert nodded. 'But first you look like you need a good hearty hot meal and a rest.'

The two men walked off to where Cuthbert was billeted. Just at that moment another man rode towards the town entrance along with his entourage. He was of Royal personage and was someone King Edward would be very pleased to see.

MALDON

Aldwine was woken by Edwin, who was shaking him vigorously. 'Father! You had better come quickly. There is an armed Heathen force approaching the town, seen by the lookouts a moment ago.'

'Uh? Oh no.' Aldwine was still groggy, but he had to think quickly. 'Burn the east and west bridges and light the beacon.'

'Already being done.'

'Is there time to get the animals inside?'

'No, too late, I fear. They are upon us. Edgar sent two of our men across the river in the canoe to get help.'

'Have they been seen?'

'I'm not sure, I am hoping not.'

'We must get every able-bodied man armed and to the palisade.'

As Aldwine and Edwin looked over their sturdy wooden wall they could see the Viking force already surrounding the outer ditch. Inside, men came running out of their houses with shields, spears and bows and arrows.

'Ask the women to gather pails of water and distribute

them around the palisade. They may try to burn it down. The men must not waste their spears. Only use them if it is a sure kill. Ask the fletcher, the carpenter and the ironsmith to start producing as many arrows and spears as they can.'

Edgar appeared from the north side of the burh.

'Any luck, Edgar?'

'Yes. The scouts were seen by the Vikings, but too late. By the time they gave chase our men had landed and escaped into the woods.'

'Well, here's hoping...'

The Vikings manoeuvred into place around the burh, bringing up a couple of carts they had robbed and pitching tents behind their lines. They ushered the captured animals into a field further away. Then, for quite a while nothing much happened, except the occasional arrow or spear being launched by either side when it looked as if a good chance of picking off a man presented itself.

'Looks like they are weighing up the situation, Father.'

But just as he finished his last word, a sudden cry went up from the invading forces and several teams of about six men charged towards the ditch with long planks of wood in an attempt to get across.

The defenders reigned spears down into the leading men in each team and a number of Vikings fell. A few more spears, arrows and stones from slings sent a few of the teams back. A couple of teams managed to cross, but scrambling up the bank, they were easy targets for the Saxon spears and eventually the raiding teams all fell back.

'First blood to us.'

Again a period of relative inactivity whilst, Edwin thought, they planned their next move. They bought up a captured Saxon farmer to the front lines and Aldwine knew what was coming. He beckoned to one of his Saxon bowman, the best archer in the town, and gave him instructions.

As the bowman loaded his arrow the poor farmer was butchered by one of the Viking warriors, who cut his throat. The arrow let fly and with deadly accuracy pierced straight through the neck of the executioner, who dropped like a stone. A defiant cheer went up from the Saxon men surrounding the bowman, shaking their fists at the invading onlookers.

Sometime later, a line of men came to the front with bows and spearman came behind them. Once again Aldwine anticipated their next move. 'Shields,' he shouted. And the Maldon men raised their large round shields above them so that the oncoming shower of arrows and spears fell onto them. The Saxon women gathered up the arrows and spears.

As darkness fell, Aldwine organised the night-watch. 'Half the men must stay on the palisade on duty. The other half sleep for four hours, then we will swap them around.'

'Yes, Father. You get some sleep too. Edgar and I will stay up. We will come and get you if need be.'

The men watched the Vikings carefully. Some too seem to retire to the tents to sleep and others sat around the fires that cooked some of the captured animals. Inside the town, Edith arranged a band of women, including Golderon and Mildryth, to distribute bowls of broth to the men.

Then, just before the changeover, the Vikings suddenly came forward and released burning arrows towards the wooden palisade. Once again the defenders were ready. Edith and some of the women, along with some of the men coming onto the night-watch, immediately grabbed the pails of water to dowse the flames. Edwin half expected another attempt by the Vikings to breach the walls, but surprisingly nothing came. Luckily the rest of the night proved uneventful.

The next morning, as dawn broke and just as the sun appeared over the horizon, three more longboats full of men appeared from the direction of the river estuary. Aldwine, looking into the glare of the rising sun, couldn't make out who they were, as they appeared only as silhouettes in a misty panorama. But as they got nearer, Aldwine's heart sank. A hundred or so armed Vikings disembarked from the ships and began to join the invading force.

Aldwine shuddered. He turned to Edwin. 'What is our food situation, my son?'

'Not good, but we can last longer, put everyone on rations.'

Aldwine sighed. 'We may have come to the point where we should try to negotiate terms with the Pagans. Our food is low and we are gradually losing our men. If they breach our walls it could be carnage. Perhaps we should surrender now and pray to God for mercy.'

He looked up at his son but was puzzled by the broad smile that suddenly appeared on Edwin's face.

'I wouldn't do that if I were you, Father. Look what's coming!'

Aldwine turned to look behind him. Over the palisade fence he could see, along the road from the west, hoards of Saxon riders galloping towards them. Behind were clouds of dust indicating wagons and carts of a marching army.

A loud cheer went up from the fort. Aldwine's face of anxiety turned to one of joy. He slapped Edwin on the back. 'Reprieved, and just in time, I reckon.'

As the mounted men rode in nearer, the Vikings started to run towards their longships, moored just east of the fortifications. Most were able to get aboard and they started fiercely paddling. A few stragglers who were slower to move or furthest from the river, were engulfed by the cavalry, who cut them to pieces then dismounted and fired arrows into the last longship, which was overcrowded with men and took some losses.

The horsemen appeared at the gates and a young, very well-dressed man appeared to lead two of his thegns into the town.

'Who is that?'

'Not sure, Father. He's very young, whoever he is. Can't be more than sixteen or seventeen.'

They hurried to meet him and Edwin recognised a royal crest on the banner carried by one of the thanes. He bowed to the young man.

'Sire?'

'I am Alfweard, son of King Edward. My father sends you his greetings.'

Of course. But it had been some time since Edwin had seen Alfweard at Winchester. Then he was just a little lad and he had grown somewhat since.

'My Lord, I am Aldwine, the reeve of the town. We can't thank you enough for your timely intervention. Where have you come from?'

'We have been at Colchester with the King. Your scouts arrived with the news of the Pagan assault on the town. My father gave orders to assemble a force and we came as fast as we could.'

'Thank God. It is such a relief. But we only held out thanks to the excellent improvements to the fortifications here that the King put into place last year.'

Alfweard smiled. 'I am glad to see his hard work has paid off.'

Just then another familiar face suddenly appeared. Cuthbert rode in, much to the delight of Edwin and Aldwine. Alongside him was a scruffy-looking teenage lad, who jumped off his horse and asked, 'Where is Mildryth?'

'Galan?' Mildryth pushed the men in front of her aside. 'Oh, thanks be to God, it *is* you.' She ran up to her brother and threw her arms around him. Both of them sobbed.

'Oh… How you have grown.'

'And Golderon? Cuthbert said she is back here.'

'Oh yes, she will be so glad to see you. What happened, Galan? We thought you were dead.'

Galan sighed. 'Let's eat and drink first, and celebrate. Then I will tell you everything.'

After another tearful re-union with Golderon, they all sat around the table with Galan's two sisters sitting close either side of him. After they all had eaten, Galan began his story.

'I saw them kill my father.' He shuddered as he recalled the moment. 'I had no idea where Mildryth was, but I was taken to the longship and tied with a rope chain to two others they had captured, both friends of mine. I was very scared for my future. We sailed along the south coast for many days. Although I hate the Pagans, and there is good reason to do so, I have to admire their navigation and sailing skills. We encountered all weather, wind, rain and rough seas. And sometimes, during a headwind, I had to row. After what seemed an eternity, we eventually landed in Ireland. I was a slave to the Irish Viking migrants who had settled there and I spent my days digging peat or sometimes ploughing the fields for them. I was locked up at night and this went on for about four years. The days were long and we worked nearly every day, only having a rest day when there was a Viking festival or day of celebration. I think I would have gone mad if it hadn't been for my Saxon compatriots and companions.

'Then, suddenly, the Vikings I worked for were attacked by a rival force and we were driven out. We sailed to England, where we were forced to march with them across Mercia to York, where I was sold to a Viking family. The work was easier, but the Viking head of the household could be cruel, especially when he got drunk, and he would beat me with a stick. Then one day he died and I was left with the mother and her daughter, who treated me well, and I suppose she had become quite fond of me. But then she married a Danish warrior. Only weeks after her marriage he was captured by a Saxon force from northern Northumbria.

'Negotiations took place between the two forces and the Vikings offered me in exchange for the warrior's return. The Saxon force did not think this was a very favourable deal and wanted money. In the end there was a compromise and money was handed over and I was exchanged as a bonus.

'The Saxon people had no particular interest in me but allowed me to go my own way. They gave me a few silver pennies and some food to see me on my way. So I started to make my way on foot heading south. I journeyed through Mercia when I heard from other travellers that all over England the Danish forces were surrendering to King Edward and that Bedford was in his hands. So that is where I headed, asking the way and carefully making a detour around the Pagan towns, as I had no wish to be in their company. Sometimes I had to beg for food from local farmers, and just before I reached Bedford I helped an elderly farmer when his cart got stuck in the mud. He gave me a few days' paid work and food and shelter. I rested a while then I heard that the King was heading for Colchester, just a short journey from my hometown. When I got there, as you know, the King and his men had chased the Pagans out of the town, and soon after arriving, I met Cuthbert, a name I had remembered from when I was little. You looked after me, didn't you, Cuthbert? But after we sat down and started talking, it wasn't long before we both realised that my sisters and his brothers were couples.'

Cuthbert continued the story. 'Yes, I asked the King if I could immediately take Galan to Maldon. King Edward told us that two men had just arrived after escaping from the besieged town. I could accompany his son and his rescue force and show him the quickest route.'

'The King has the utmost respect for you, Cuthbert. He orders everyone around, as a King must, but it is as though he *asks* Cuthbert rather than demands of him.'

Cuthbert looked sheepish. 'He knows I will do anything for him. I enjoy the job I do for him. I feel it is worthwhile and helpful to the King. I think he is a good man and a great King, fair but tough when he needs to be. He wants to bring law and order to these kingdoms.'

'And he didn't want you in the thick of the fighting either. Which is why we were in the rear of the warriors following Lord Alfweard. Anyway, I can't tell you all how good it is to be back home after all these years. I can help with any repairs in the town tomorrow.'

'You will do no such thing!' exclaimed Mildryth. 'You will have at least seven full days' rest before you do anything at all. You need it.'

Galan smiled at his sister. 'You always were a bossyboots.'

Everyone laughed and Mildryth opened her mouth as if shocked. She kissed her brother on the cheek and they gave each other a big hug.

A few days later Cuthbert was summoned to the King and given instructions to travel to Gloucester. Edward was scheming and making future plans. 'Tell our Lady Athelflaed that we need to meet before the year is out. Actually, invite her and Athelstan to come and meet me at Winchester for Yule celebrations but let her know that I will be holding an important secret meeting to discuss our ventures and intentions for next year.'

'Yes, My Lord.' And within an hour Cuthbert had packed provisions and was on his way riding out westwards towards Gloucester.

Many candles lit up the hall, throwing long shadows across the room. It was cold outside and a good fire was burning with Edward sitting close. Alongside him around a small table were his two sons, his brother and his sister. Guards had been posted on the door with strict instructions that they were not to be disturbed under any circumstances.

Saxon Essex

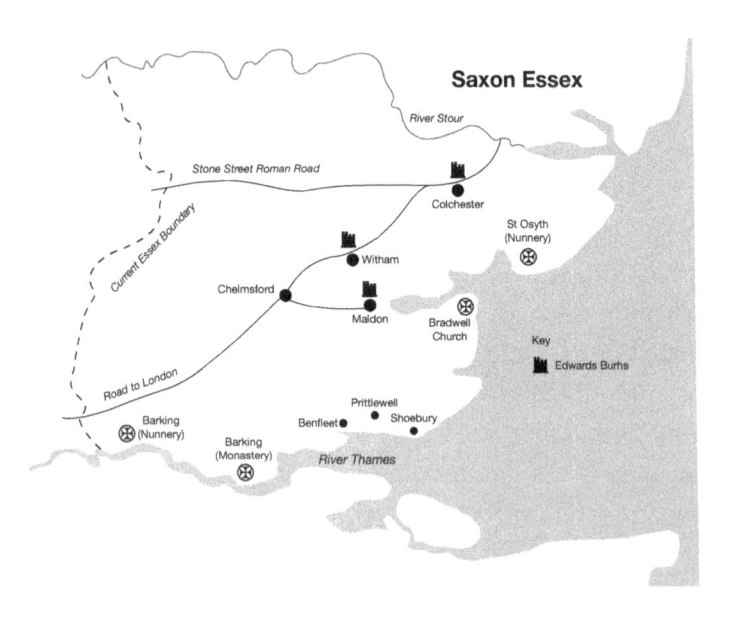

River Stour

Stone Street Roman Road

Current Essex Boundary

Colchester

Witham

Chelmsford

Maldon

St Osyth (Nunnery)

Bradwell Church

Key

Edwards Burhs

Road to London

Prittlewell

Benfleet   Shoebury

Barking (Nunnery)

Barking (Monastery)

River Thames

WINCHESTER

'I am glad you could make the journey, sister. You look a little tired.'

'I feel okay. You, my dear brother, look more and more like our father every time I see you.'

'You think so? Well, I often think of him and I hope we have done him proud. We have fortified our Saxon towns on the borders of our lands and the Danelaw lands agreed by him and Guthrum. We are now in a much stronger position, and we have control of Essex and most of East Anglia. Your agreement a few years ago, Athelflaed, with Owain of Strathclyde and Constantine of Scotland to ally against the Pagans, was a shrewd move. Do you think it still stands?'

'Oh yes, I don't think the Scots will be interfering with any plans we have in Mercia.'

'Good. Then it is time to move to the next stage of our plan: a strike against the five boroughs in Danish Mercia. I will need your help, sister. We must co-ordinate our attack together so that two armies confront the Danish towns at the same time.'

Athelflaed nodded. 'I like the sound of this. The time of reckoning has come.'

'If you make an assault on Derby and then Leicester, I will deal with Stamford and then Nottingham. That just leaves Lincoln. Once that is taken, virtually all of Mercia will be back in our hands.'

'What opposition are you expecting? Will they submit without a fight?' Athelstan's piercing blue eyes looked to his aunt and father in turn.

'That is the hope, my son, but I doubt if we could expect

to take control of these without a conflict somewhere along the line.'

'And what of the kingdom of Northumbria?' enquired Alfweard.

'I think that is for another day. Ragnall, the Dane who controls York, is a tough warrior, but I think he has his own problems. Eh, sister?'

'Quite so, brother. The southern region of Deira is controlled by Ragnall, but northern Bernicia is contested by the Saxon Ealdred of Bamburgh, who still has much influence there and likes to call himself King.'

'You know Ealdred well enough, don't you, Father?'

'Well, I have met him only once, but his father and King Alfred were good friends.'

'I think, brother, Ealdred is looking for an alliance with Constantine, as he could not tackle Ragnall on his own. His army and a Scottish force would be an even match against Ragnall's formidable army. Anyway, a conflict between them is inevitable.'

'So Northumbria is no great threat to us presently. Which just leaves Wales. But once again, Athelflaed, we have you to thank for keeping them quiet.'

'Well, last year I was incensed by the murder of Abbott Egberht, whom I had sent out as a missionary into Brycheniog, where King Tewdyr reigns. He may not be directly responsible, but he needs to keep his subjects in order. I personally led a force into Wales, taking thirty-four hostages, including Tewdyr's wife, forcing him to submit.'

'And, it seems, giving a warning to all the Welsh magnates, who have been somewhat restrained ever since.'

'So when do we spring into action, Edward?'

'I propose next summer.' He turned to his brother. 'I will take Alfweard with me, but I trust you can look after things here in Winchester again, Athelweard.'

'Most definitely. What about our council, Edward? You will be calling the Witans of Wessex and Mercia?'

'Absolutely. But not until shortly before we depart for battle. Maybe a few weeks before. We will listen to their advice, but I am confident that they will ultimately support us over this.'

Athelweard agreed. 'May God be with you all.'

CHAPTER 11
THE YEAR 918
TAMWORTH

Athelflaed, the Lady of the Mercians, had returned to the town of Tamworth, which she had fortified five years earlier. Athelhun, the Bishop of Worcester, who had succeeded Werferth, was there to greet her. She entered the house next to the church and threw down her sword. Then she took off her armour and sat down on a stool, exhausted. Her maid wrapped a cloak around her.

'Where is my daughter?'

'Elfwyn is at church, My Lady.'

'Praying again, no doubt. She seems to do a lot of that.' The bishop said nothing but ventured a thin smile. 'And Athelstan?'

'I will try and find out, My Lady. I believe he has just returned with his men from skirmishing with the Pagans around York.'

'Brave of him to venture into Northumbria. But then again, he was never short of courage. Just like his father.'

Athelflaed removed her boots and, with a sigh, sat on a thick rug with cushions and pillows.

Moments later Athelstan appeared and sat down with his aunt.

'Oh, Athelstan I feel so weary. I have such a pain in my head.' She noticed that her nephew had a hint of a smile and a rather smug look on his face. 'And what are you looking so pleased about?'

'Well, dear aunt, I have news. On my return from Tadcaster I met a week ago with one of Ragnall's envoys. He has declared that his Viking King is prepared to meet with you and accept you as overlord. Overlady in this case, I suppose.'

'Really? I wonder what prompted this.'

'Ah, well, the King is approaching from Stamford, and with Derby and Leicester finally submitting to you, he is virtually surrounded. I think he has no stomach for a battle. The result would be inevitable.'

Athelflaed looked pensive. 'I suppose so. I am glad Leicester surrendered without a fight. Derby was not so easy. We lost some very good men there, Athelstan. After all the battles and the conflict with these Pagans, I hope God will forgive me for sacrificing all the Saxon men that have died for our cause.'

'There was not a man who was not willing to fight for you, Aunt. Much has been achieved and some without any blood being shed, thanks to your gift of diplomacy. Even my father can learn something there, I think.'

'Well, maybe. I must retire. I do not feel so good tonight. Would you tell the maid to bring me a drink?'

'Of course. Goodnight, Aunt.'

The maid took her mistress a drink. She later checked on her to find that she had fallen asleep, her left arm stretched out to one side. She blew out the candles and drew a curtain around her.

The next morning there was a clear blue sky with not a cloud to be seen. Even from early in the day, there was a heat haze that indicated it was going to be a scorching hot day. Athelstan had already left with the local fyrd and some of his own men to secure more of the land for the Saxons.

The maid had waited for Athelflaed to appear, but time ticked by and there was no movement from the bed. 'I will take Our Lady a glass of milk and some bread and butter,' she declared to one of the other servants.

She drew back the drape in front of the bed, keeping the tray steady with the other hand. 'My Lady... My Lady? Oh no!'

The tray and its contents crashed to the floor and the maid put her hands to her face. There was a blank expression on Athelflaed's face and an equally blank stare towards the ceiling. Her body was in exactly the same position it had been when the maid had left her the evening before with her arm out to one side. She screamed for the bishop, who hurried in only to see Athelflaed's lifeless body before him. He closed her eyes and, taking off a large wooden cross that hung about his neck, he placed it on the body of His Lady.

'A shock. We must recall Athelstan immediately and send an urgent message to the King that Our Lady has died during the night. They will both be devastated.'

'As will Our Lady Elfwyn. I will find her and tell her the

news so that she can pray for her mother's soul.' The bishop nodded and the tearful maid ran out to locate Athelflaed's daughter.

The scouts were immediately sent out. The news of her death spread rapidly in Tamworth. The bishop decided to pull up the burh drawbridge and guard the entrances to the town for safekeeping.

On the afternoon of the next day, Cuthbert appeared, having ridden the sixty miles from Stamford almost nonstop. The guards, when they realised who he was and that he wore the badge of the King's messenger, let him in immediately.

He entered the house where Bishop Athelhun and Athelstan were sat in conversation. 'Welcome, Cuthbert. Has my father been informed of our sad news?'

'Yes, Sire. He immediately set off from Stamford with only six men. He will stay in Leicester tonight and be here tomorrow.'

'I hope he will be impressed by the recent fortifications my aunt and I have constructed there.'

'Do you need to send me to send a message to him there, My Lord?'

'No, Cuthbert. As usual you have carried out your instructions dutifully and deserve a rest and a hot meal. We will await the King's arrival.' He beckoned to one of the servants to help Cuthbert with his horse and to provide him with sustenance.

The next day Edward, upon his arrival, promptly arranged a meeting with all the prominent people who could be present.

They sat around a large round table, not unlike the one at Winchester. Before the King could speak Athelhun offered his condolences.

'Thank you, Bishop. Now, we must arrange for Athelflaed's body to be taken to her Priory of St Oswald, where her husband lay buried and which she founded with him twenty years ago. Elfwyn can accompany her on the journey to Gloucester. As a member of the Witan, Bishop, have you been able to summon the members to gather for council?'

'Yes, My Lord. But, um...'

'Yes? What is it?'

'Well, I don't think they will accept Elfwyn as Our Lady of Mercia's successor.'

'Yes, I think my thoughts were similar. Leave Elfwyn to me.'

'I will arrange for Aunt's tomb to be made,' declared Athelstan. 'Exactly where are the relics of St Oswald that Our Lady recovered from the Pagans?'

This raised a smile from all around. In the year 909 Athelflaed had conjured up a daring plan, with Edward's help, to venture into Viking territory in Lincolnshire and successfully steal back from under their noses the bones of the seventh-century King of Northumbria who had been venerated as a saint, and the priory was dedicated to him.

The bishop could not be precise. 'The monks keep it in a private and secure part of the priory.'

Edward stood up to stretch his legs. 'I am pleased to say that Stamford, previously one of the five Danelaw boroughs, is now in our hands. Though mostly populated by the Vikings, there has been efforts there to convert the Pagan people to Christians. Nottingham is another borough that has submitted to us, but before I make my way to Gloucester I need to secure a burgh there and man it with loyal Saxon thegns and men. Then I will come back for the burial of my beloved sister.'

'All of East Anglia and Essex is under your rule, Father. You have made wonderful progress.'

'With your help, my son, and your aunt.'

'And the Witan will very likely wish you, My Lord, to be ruler of Mercia as well as Essex.'

'I will rely on your support, Bishop, to fix this. We need to secure the kingdom as soon as possible so that the Vikings cannot take advantage of an unstable situation.'

'Does Athelweard know what has happened?'

'I have sent Cuthbert to Winchester to tell him. He can join us in Gloucester later. Now, I need to speak to Elfwyn.'

Elfwyn had a private audience with Edward. She spoke first. 'What will happen now, Uncle? Am I to try to rule Mercia?'

The anxious look on her face spoke volumes to Edward. But he wanted to be gentle with his niece. 'Do you think you could?'

'Not really. I am not like my mother. I do not have the aptitude for administration and certainly not for battle as she did.'

'Your mother was an exceptional woman. Almost never has Mercia or any other kingdom in England had a woman as ruler.'

'But what is to become of me?'

'Why don't you come to Gloucester and join the nuns at the Priory of St Oswald? Later, if you so wish, you can stay at

Winchester and join the order there, at St Mary's Abbey. You already have a good relationship with your Uncle Athelweard and his two sons who spend most of their time there.'

'The Nunnaminster my grandmother founded?'

'Yes, it is much more than just a place of prayer. It has become a centre of much learning, culture and art. My mother would be very pleased to think that her granddaughter would spend her days there. I will escort you there after we celebrate you mother's burial at Gloucester.'

Elfwyn pondered for a moment. 'Yes. I think I would like that. And will you rule Mercia… or Athelstan, maybe?'

'By being ruler of Wessex and Mercia we can unite these two great kingdoms, perhaps forever. And I am not a young man anymore. Who knows how much time I have left, but Athelstan is already prepared to take over from me.'

'God protect us all.'

CANTERBURY (CANTWAREBURH)

Edward stood in the Great Hall next to the cathedral in Canterbury. He was restless and fidgety, waiting for his eldest daughter Eadgifu to appear with her eleven-year-old sister Eadhild. Alongside him was Plegmund.

The King sighed.

'Patience, my King, this is a big moment for her. It is not every day a lady is to be married.'

'Yes, of course. From the size of the chest she brought from Winchester, if she tries all her dresses on, we could be here for some time.'

But at that moment his teenage daughter appeared in a long white gown of satin with gold trim and a gold belt.

Eadgifu was tall with long, chestnut-coloured hair which curled around her shoulders. She stood with her sister before her father, who smiled at the sight of her.

'You look beautiful! Doesn't she, Archbishop?'

'Oh yes, wonderful.'

'Well, I hope my future husband thinks so, Father. What, may I ask, is the schedule for tomorrow?'

'Ah, well, King Charles has already set sail from Francia and should be in Dover by now. Thegn Edmund and Cuthbert are there to meet him and show the way to Canterbury. He is due to arrive here around midday tomorrow.'

'And so what will be my title? Queen of the West Franks?'

'Yes, I presume. Archbishop Plegmund here will give you a blessing and then we will feast before you depart to Francia and your wedding will take place there in a few weeks' time. Would that be at Reims, Archbishop?'

'I would think so.'

Eadgifu puffed out her cheeks. 'Suppose I don't like him or I am not attracted to him?'

'I hear he is quite a handsome and charming man.'

'And what are your marriage plans for me, Father?' Eadhild piped up. Daughters of kings knew that, unless they entered the Church, marriages were usually arranged for convenience and foreign alliances.

'You are still young, my little one. Nothing is arranged yet.'

'We heard that you were negotiating with Hugh, the Duke of the Franks.'

Edward raised his eyebrows. 'You two are well informed. Well, as I said, there is nothing arranged yet. Now, this afternoon I have to make a visit to a young lady. I cannot say too much.'

'You don't need to, Father. We all know that you intend to go and see my namesake, Eadgifu of Kent. You have had a thing about her for years.'

Edward put his hands on his hips. 'Great saints! Is there nothing you don't know? Where in heavens do you get your information?'

The two sisters looked at each other and giggled. Edward glanced sideways at his archbishop, who shrugged and suddenly made a quick exit. Eadgifu put her arms around the waist of her father. His stern look changed and he gave a brief chuckle, returning the hug.

Edward stole out into the cold November evening wrapped up in a thick cloak. He arrived at the agreed meeting place with Eadgifu of Kent. The archbishop tried to persuade the King that he should be accompanied, but Edward insisted that he go alone, disguised and in secret.

Suddenly she appeared with her maid, who discreetly stayed in the background. Eadgifu had long golden hair and wore a long green gown. Her beauty was renowned and she had many admirers, but none so eminent as the King. She had no telling expression on her face.

'I thank you for coming, Eadgifu. Further to our meeting at Winchester last year, have you resolved your land dispute with Goda and your estates at Coolling?'

Eadgifu nodded.

'Um… Look, I will come straight to the point, as my time is limited.' He hesitated. '…marry me.'

There was no change on the deadpan face of Eadgifu.

'But, My Lord, I thought you were already married.'

'She... Aelfflaed has taken sanctuary in the nunnery at Wilton. She has decided to retreat from public life.'

'And why would I want to marry a man who is twice my age when there are many more who are younger and more handsome?' Eadgifu suppressed a smile.

Edward frowned, hurt from her comment. 'I can give you a good life in Winchester. Anything you desire. Land, property and riches.'

'I already have those things.'

Edward's frustration began to show. 'But you know how I feel about you.' Edward put his arm around her waist and kissed her on the cheek. Still no change in expression. 'You are headstrong like your father, Sigehelm.'

'I was too small to remember him. But I heard he was bad-tempered, argumentative and stubborn.'

'But loyal to the Saxon cause and a great leader. I shall remain forever indebted to him for his brave action at the Battle of the Holme and the demise of Athelwold.'

'Yes, so I would be the wife of a warrior king always at war with Vikings, never at home and leaving a wife always vulnerable to being a widow.'

'I can leave the fighting to Athelstan. I need to spend more time at home. And you could be the mother of kings.'

'You already have three living sons. And stepmother to... how many children now?'

'Look, Eadgifu, life could be exciting. Would you be happy with a mundane life in Kent?'

She looked into the King's eyes. There was a hint of a smile. Edward kissed her, expecting her to pull away, but she allowed it.

'Take a while to think about it, and if you accept then come to the archbishop's house after the King of the Franks has left on Wodensday.'

The following day, the King's daughter stood nervously with her father in the hall, as she listened to the approaching marching band of the Frankish escort to the King of the West Franks. The two kings had never met before. A fanfare sounded. Charles entered the building and bowed to Edward, who returned with the same. 'It is a great pleasure to welcome you here, Charles.'

'The pleasure is all mine, Edward.' Charles looked at Eadgifu and smiled. She looked somewhat relieved. *He has a nice smile*, she thought. Although in his late thirties, he was still a reasonably handsome man with a neat moustache and beard and long dark hair. Charles took Eadgifu's hand and kissed it. 'I know such Royal arranged marriages are awkward, my dear, but I hope in time this will prove to be fruitful and a good match.'

Eadgifu smiled. Edward showed his guest to the seat by the fire. 'We will feast and celebrate for the next day.'

Food was brought in on large platters and all the guests ate and drank. After some small talk and polite exchange of gifts, Edward indulged in some more serious talk with Charles, who was a fellow Christian.

'The Pagan threat from the Norsemen seems to go on endlessly, Charles. It is a constant battle.'

'Yes, I confess we have had our own problems.'

'So this Viking called Rollo. I understand you have given him land and come to some agreement.'

'That is so. We have given him land in Normandy in

exchange for peace and protection against further Viking raids. He accepts me as overlord and has promised to pay for some of the land… though I doubt I will ever get it.'

'Do you trust him?'

'I don't have much choice really. I have my own problems with the King of the East Franks. I see trouble ahead.'

'But you have secured the kingdom of Lotharingia which lies betwixt the two, and you are king there now.'

Charles nodded. 'I managed to secure good support there, helped by my marriage to my last wife, who died last year. She was, of course, from Lotharingia. Also, I have married my niece to one of their nobles. But even with their support, I can see war with the East Franks. It might be that Rollo can even be my ally in this conflict. Although he seems content to be left alone and build up his own separate state in Normandy, having no wish to stay connected to the Vikings from his homeland. He has been baptised and so he has become a Christian and even calls himself a Norman rather than a Viking. In fact, he calls himself Duke of Normandy. I may try to secure a marriage between one of my daughters and Rollo, or, if that is not possible, his son.'

'Mmm, I see. I hope the Normans do not cause you problems then. We both have to fight hard to secure our kingdoms. But on a more personal issue, do you intend to have children with Eadgifu?'

'Oh yes, I would love it if she was to provide me with a son. I have six children from my last marriage, all of them girls! The eldest is only ten years old so I am hoping Eadgifu will have a good relationship with them as a stepmother. They are quite a handful, those girls.'

'I can imagine. My last marriage provided me with six

daughters too. I think the girls are much more troublesome than the boys!' They both laughed.

When it was time to leave the following day, Eadgifu bade a tearful farewell to her father and Edward wished Charles good luck with all his endeavours. The Franks left with the same flourish of fanfare as when they arrived. Edward was left wondering whether he would ever see his daughter again and was gazing at the door of the hall, which had been left ajar, letting in the cold air. Just then through the door arrived Eadgifu of Kent.

Edward's eyes lit up. 'Eadgifu. Everyone has just left.'

'I know. I waited until they had gone.'

'You… Does this mean…?'

Eadgifu smiled. 'I must be mad. But then again, who could refuse such a gracious and gallant king?' She went to Edward and embraced him tenderly.

CHAPTER 12
THE YEAR 920
BAKEWELL

Edward looked with satisfaction at the fortifications, which were now completed. Bakewell, in the beautiful rolling hills and countryside thirty miles north of Derby, had a burh with a deep ditch and rampart and a good wooden palisade all the way around it. The King would occupy it with reliable Saxon men led by two local thegns, although the existing Viking families who had been there for some years would be staying on and would hopefully live in harmony with the Saxon soldiers and their families.

This followed on from the previous visit by Edward, where even greater defences had been constructed by many men at Nottingham, the previously Viking town in the heart of the Danelaw. Two burhs now stood on either side of the River Trent and a new bridge across the river between the two.

At Bakewell a new hall had also been built to accommodate the coming visitors. This was a momentous time for Edward and the House of Wessex. Envoys from Wales and the Scottish King would be arriving tomorrow to pay homage to Edward and accept him as overlord and father to their nation. Today, Ragnall, the self-styled King and Viking leader in York, would be doing the same, making a personal appearance. Also, the King of Strathclyde.

The King had summoned many of the Saxon nobility and high churchmen to witness the treaties and the charters that were about to be signed. His sons Athelstan and Alfweard were there, as well as his brother Athelweard. Frithestan, the Bishop of Winchester, had administered the writing of several documents and had run over the content and wording with the King.

'This is to make Maldon a borough, Sire. And these other two are what we discussed earlier and just require the signatures.'

'Thank you. Athelweard, please come and sign as witness. I will sign as "*King of the English*".'

At that moment, just as Edward had finished signing, a horn sounded, signalling the arrival of Ragnall and his entourage. Edward went to the door. The old Viking warrior was helped down from his horse by one of his earls. As he approached, wrapped in a heavy woollen cloak, Edward could see he was a big man, broad and tall with a long beard and piercing blue eyes. There was an old battle scar on the left side of his face and he looked weary, and probably, Edward estimated, a little older than himself.

Ragnall bowed and greeted Edward with a handshake. 'My Lord. We meet at last.'

'Welcome, Ragnall. How was your journey from York?'

'Longer than I thought. I feel rather tired.'

'We will eat and drink shortly. Come and meet my family.'

After the introductions the two kings sat down with a goblet of wine. In the middle of the hall a wild boar was cooking over the fire.

Ragnall sat back in his chair. 'I have something for you, Edward.' He beckoned his earl to bring over a small chest and open it in front of them. In it were gleaming gold and silver coins.

Edward picked up a handful. 'A generous gift. I see your own head is featured on these coins.'

'Yes, minted in York.'

'You were about to make a treaty with my sister, the Lady of Mercia, when the negotiations were interrupted by her untimely death.'

'Yes, quite a woman, your sister. Fearsome when she had to be. Nothing much to negotiate. She would be patron providing I could remain King and reside in York. I presumed that as you were now the King of Mercia as well as Wessex, the arrangement could be the same.'

'Yes, something along similar lines. I have a treaty for you to sign. But realise, Ragnall, that I am now master in virtually all of southern England, Essex and East Anglia, and tomorrow will be receiving homage from the Welsh and the King of Scotland.'

Ragnall smiled. 'You have done well, Edward. And do you have ambitions to rule in Northumbria too?'

Edward laughed. 'Well, maybe one day.' He raised his eyebrows at Ragnall. 'But I think I am getting too old for all this fighting nonsense. I think I need some peace and quiet these days.'

'My feelings exactly. I need to rest my poor old bones and live the remainder of my life, however long that is, in tranquillity at York. Which is why I am very happy to accept you as overlord and live by your laws... if we can live together in peace.'

Edward was surprised. He thought Ragnall would be a rough diamond who would be difficult to deal with. But despite an unsettled life of constant battle and war, he seemed a man of some intelligence.

'Have you come to understanding with Constantine, the Scottish King? You had quite a battle with him at Corbridge.'

'Oh, him. Well, let's say that it is honours even. I won't bother him again if he accepts my authority in York.'

'And the rest of Northumbria? You have some rivalry in your cousin Sihtric and also Ealdred, the Saxon from Bamburgh.'

Ragnall folded his arms and looked down at the floor. 'Sihtric is leaving me alone at present, but I know he has designs on taking York from me if he had the chance. As for Ealdred, I know he is a friend of yours. He still has a small part of Northumbria and has the protection of Constantine. He's a survivor.'

'As are you, Ragnall. Yet you have fought everyone. Scots, Saxons the Irish and even other Vikings.'

'Well, it's true I have had to fight hard for survival. Which is why I want to retire in peace to York.'

'Why York? I am told you came from Ireland.'

'I was born and raised in Ireland, but we were continually warring with other Vikings and the Irish. I thought we were wild, but the Irish... madmen! York seems relatively... well, normal.'

'How did your family get to Ireland?'

'It was my grandfather Imar who left Norway in hope of finding a better life and sailed around Scotland to find land in Ireland. For a while all seemed satisfactory but then more Vikings arrived and encouraged local Irish tribes to drive out their Viking rivals.'

Edward was quizzical. 'So tell me, Ragnall, I need to understand. Why is it so many Vikings are anxious to leave Scandinavia and pick on these islands as their alternative?'

'You have to realise that Norway, where my grandfather came from, is a country with a cold and unfriendly climate. Its terrain is rocky with little fertile land that is fought over by rival families. There is something in the Viking blood which gives us ambitious dreams. This, along with our sometimes-aggressive nature, results in voyages to green and more pleasant lands. England and these islands are a suitable attraction. Our sailing skills allow us to sail here without having to come too far and find land and opportunity to settle, even if it means fighting for it.'

'I have battled with the Viking people all my life. You must know yourself, relentless fighting wears you out.'

'And, King, you have been a very worthy adversary. But in time Vikings and Saxons can live together. They do now in some places.'

'This would be easier if they could accept Christianity. But they seem to want to maintain their Pagan status and refuse Jesus, who guides us and sets an example of how to live.'

'Yes, but you have to remember that the Saxon people have been receptive to Christianity for hundreds of years, since Augustine reached these shores.'

'*St* Augustine,' Edward corrected Ragnall, who smiled.

'And many Vikings *have* been converted. As for me, I don't really have the time for religion. I am too old in the tooth and a lost cause.'

'Pity. Still… come and eat, Ragnall. It looks like our meal is ready. It is roast pig.'

'Excellent, I am very hungry and that sounds perfect.'

The next day, Ragnall departed with a gift of a jewelled silver cross from Edward, who was reluctant to give up his efforts to convert the Pagans to Christianity. Ragnall smiled broadly and thanked the King before returning to York. Edward watched him ride away.

Over the next week Edward received more important rulers and kings who had come to pay homage to Edward and swear allegiance to him as overlord. First, the envoys from Strathclyde representing Owain and shortly after the Welsh rulers. Then Ealdred appeared with Constantine, the King of Scotland. Edward gave Ealdred a warm welcome, then shook hands with Constantine and thanked him for coming. Then he invited them to sit with him and his two sons.

Constantine spoke first. 'There is no doubt that we both have a common aim, Sire, to defeat and repel the invading Viking forces that constantly arrive from Scandinavia. Also to keep control of the Pagan forces that already reside in our lands, especially in Northumbria, where Ragnall continues to be a threat to us.'

Edward nodded in agreement. 'I have just spoken with Ragnall. He left here a few days ago and has agreed to accept me as overlord. He has assured me that he has no intention to expand further into Northumbria and Scotland. You should be safe from any attack from him and if he breaks his word he knows I will bring the whole Saxon force against him. He is in no position to defend against my army. But there may be the arrival of further longboats bringing invading Pagan forces to your shores and mine.'

'Are you able to protect us from them in Scotland and Northumbria.'

'I cannot be everywhere at once and have my own problems, but any Viking that arrives in your kingdom who does not come in peace is our enemy as well as yours. May I suggest that the two of you remain in alliance and help each other. Obviously you are stronger together.'

Ealdred nodded. 'Bernicia, where I reside, is still very vulnerable to raids from the Danes. We suffered from the very first attacks over a hundred years ago. When they landed at the Holy Island of Lindisfarne, they plundered the church and took its riches. The invaders realised that such raids were easy pickings and the word soon spread to the Norse lands over the sea.'

'Nothing much has changed,' Edward reflected. 'But to be a little more positive, there are more and more Viking people living in peace in this land and some have adopted our Christian faith. We must endeavour to continue to persevere with their conversion. My treaty with you provides such a condition.' He beckoned to Bishop Frithestan, who presented a large scroll for the kings to sign. It spelt out the supreme authority of King Edward to which they must agree. Also, his direct rule of all the kingdoms except Northumbria. Constantine then Ealdred signed their names and it was witnessed by the other members of Edward's Royal family. Further conversation took place long into the evening before they all celebrated a great feast.

England in 920

- Lands where Edward is Overlord
- Lands under Edwards direct rule
- ▲ Five Boroughs of the Daneland

SCOTLAND (Constantine)

STRATHCLYDE (Owain)

Bernicia (Ealdred)

NORTHUMBRIA

Deira (Ragnall)

York

Chester

Bakewell

▲ Lincoln

▲ Derby ▲ Nottingham

Tamworth

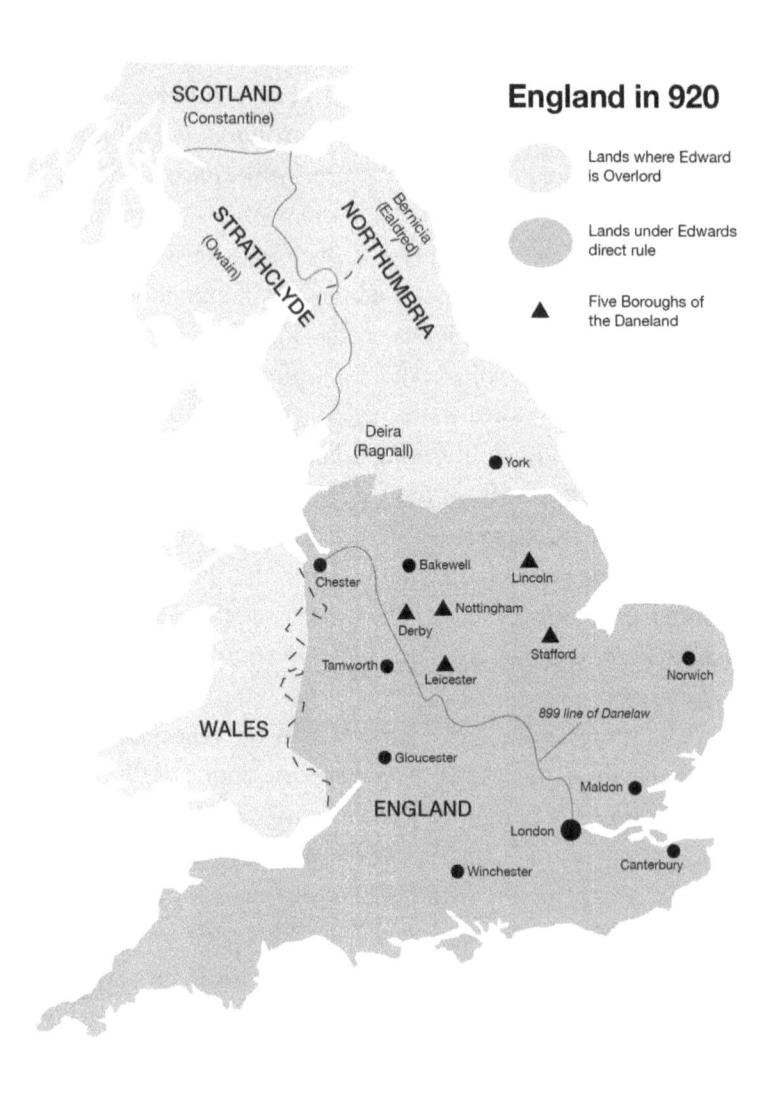

▲ Leicester Stafford

Norwich

WALES

899 line of Danelaw

Gloucester

Maldon

ENGLAND

London

Winchester Canterbury

MALDON

It was the annual tournament organised by Edwin, who was adjudicator. There was archery, sword fighting, spear throwing and a climbing contest. The archery had four target bosses. Six men competed on each target. Both Edgar and Galan were doing rather well and had won on their respective targets. The four target winners competed in the final on one target, shooting three arrows each. Galan had shot and scored one bullseye, but one arrow had gone completely astray, only just hitting the outside of the target. Edgar was last to shoot but needed two bullseyes to beat the village champion. His first shot was just outside the bullseye, but the second was bang in the middle. He needed one more. He carefully eased back his bow and took careful aim. He let fly and watched as the arrow hit the target. It looked very close to the line but unfortunately just outside the bullseye. The marshal rushed up to look but shook his head.

Edgar was runner-up.

There was also a junior and a ladies' archery contest. Mildryth had entered the ladies and won the competition!

She went up to her husband. 'Bad luck, Edgar. You were so close.'

'Bit embarrassing that my wife is a better shot than I am!'

Mildryth laughed. 'Well, we were a bit nearer than the men.'

In the spear throwing, each man had three throws and it was a simple matter of who could throw the furthest. Galan was narrowly winning. He had gained immense strength from digging the Irish peat bogs when he was a slave. On his last throw he had mastered the technique and the angle of flight. The spear flew and flew. It looked like it would never come down and the crown stood with open mouths in awe.

'By the saints! I have never seen a spear thrown that far by anyone,' declared Edwin. 'He is a clear winner.'

Galan, puffed up with pride, grinned broadly.

Next was the climbing contest, which consisted of getting to the top of a tall tree on the edge of the village and ringing the bell at the top of the trunk, by heaving an axe in each hand into the trunk and edging up to the top. It needed immense strength but also skill. If you dug the axes in too far they were difficult to remove. If they were not in far enough they may dislodge as the climber put his weight on it, and there were grimaces and groans when a number of climbers fell off the trunk onto the straw stacked up around the base of the trunk.

Each contestant was allowed two goes. Galan's second go proved unbeatable. Once again his arm and superior shoulder strength was impressive as he got the top of the tree in double-quick time and rang the bell.

The final contest was the sword fighting. This was not Galan's forte and he did not even make the last eight. But Edgar was regarded as a fine swordsman and sure enough, he was in the final bout. With blunted swords the two battled for several minutes until Edgar's opponent lunged at him, but as Edgar neatly sidestepped, his opponent lost his balance and fell, exhausted. The two men shook hands.

Each winner was given a prize, which was the weapon of the contest, so Galan was given an axe and a spear both of the highest quality. Edwin was given a beautiful sword and Mildryth a yew bow which made her very proud.

But it was Galan who was declared the village champion.

He had won two competitions and got to the final of the archery. He was awarded a new gold coin. A few of the pretty girls of the village went up to him to congratulate him and asked to see the shiny gold coin.

Then the village gathered round for the outdoor feast, where much mead was drank. It was the village recipe, which fermented honey with spices and hops and had a high alcoholic content. Many of the villagers had contributed to donating the food and the celebrations went long into the evening. When it began to get dark, the children were sent to bed and a large fire was lit where the villagers gathered round and chatted. Very sadly, Edith was not there. She was tending to Aldwine, who, unbeknown to the rest of his family, who thought he was just under the weather, lay dying in his house.

Several weeks later, on a beautiful September afternoon, Edwin sat looking out over the River Blackwater, cradling his young one-year-old son in his arms. There was a gentle breeze blowing and the trees overhanging the far riverbank were reflected in the water. A fishing boat had anchored out in the middle of the river and the men were casting their nets whilst the children were dangling their lines and hooks over the side.

Then four longboats could be seen sailing towards them. But these were not Viking invaders but Saxon ships. Maldon had become an important port along the east coast. A place where trading ships could moor up and where the King's English fleet could dock as a stopover on their way around the coast. Edwin watched as the ships pulled down their sails and their skilful oarsmen manoeuvred onto the new jetty which King Edward had ordered to be constructed.

His whole family was with him, mucking about by the river. Agnar was now an energetic ten-year-old, a blond tearaway, wrestling with his cousin, Edgar's oldest son. Golderon was showing their seven-year-old daughter how to sew and Edwin's five-year-old son was throwing stones into the river. Edith arrived with a basket of apples to hand around to her grandchildren.

Edwin smiled at his mother, but his feelings were a mixture of contentment, pride and sadness. Sadness, because his father hasd sadly passed away the previous week. The town had voted Edwin as the leader and reeve of the town, which had been endorsed by the King.

In fact, it was the King himself who had sent his recommendation to the town after hearing about Aldwine's death from Cuthbert. Edwin was very highly regarded by the people of Maldon as being of wise and sensible character and protective of the townsfolk. This had made him very proud. The position of reeve often went to the son of the passing elderman anyway. It was usually the eldest son, but Cuthbert was in permanent employment by the King and followed wherever the King went. He had his own residence in Winchester now but spent most of his time campaigning with the King or scouting somewhere on his behalf.

And Edwin's family had given him much satisfaction. Life in the Dengie peninsular was peaceful. But Edwin knew that this could change at any time, especially with the arrival of marauding Vikings. And who could predict what damage they could do?

CHAPTER 13
THE YEAR 924
FARNDON

The Saxon army were at the end of a long day's march and King Edward was riding at the head of the long line of men. Riding alongside him was his son Athelstan. Edward had a much longer beard now, which made him look older, and he protected his head with a shiny silver helmet. He was pondering over recent events and thinking about the future. They were returning from Chester, where the Welsh had initiated an uprising with some of the Mercian locals, no doubt bribing them or promising impossible proposals.

'Well, my son, that was the first conflict we have had to deal with recently. These last few years have been a period of relative peace and stability, which has given me much satisfaction, Just as well. I am no longer a young man. In days gone by we would have relied on Athelflaed to quell such a revolt, as she did twenty years earlier, but as she is no longer with us, it is down to us to deal with such matters.'

'Yes. I presume Alfweard is keeping watch in Winchester.'

'He is old enough to trust with such responsibility now, especially since the death of my brother.'

'It is a shame Uncle Athelweard is gone.'

'Yes, he was a good man and always helpful to me.'

But, thought Edward, *when I am gone, I really want one son to succeed me so that England will become one united kingdom and not divided by regions again as it once was. I especially want no rivalry between Wessex and Mercia.*

He knew that son would have to be Athelstan. He glanced over at his eldest child, who was now aged almost thirty and in his prime. His organisational skills were exceptional. He had proved himself in battle and he was strong and healthy. He also seemed to have a way of knowing how to deal with people, something which he no doubt learned from his aunt Athelflaed.

'Athelstan, I feel happy that the succession after I am gone is secure. I have three sons destined to outlive me and able to rule, and two more although they are just babies at the moment. I have been lucky. All my children survive and still remain here in England.'

'Yes, Father. Surprising to see my sister Eadgifu back here in England, and with her young son Louis.'

'Yes, poor Charles has many problems. He has been deposed but still hopes to restore himself to the kingdom of the West Franks. I think it is better for Eadgifu to remain here in the meantime.'

'And what is the latest news from Northumbria?'

'Well, when Ragnall died, Sihtric instantly moved into York just as Ragnall had predicted. The town has such a large Danish population, he was the only one they were prepared to accept in such circumstances.'

'But I believe Ealdred still survives in Bamburgh.'

'He does indeed, and with Constantine still supporting him, I doubt if Sihtric will dare to attack him. I have not the energy or the resources to move into Northumbria and build our Saxon burhs at the moment, but whilst they are bickering with each other, they are no threat to us.'

'My objective, Father, is to one day convert Sihtric to a Christian.'

'I commend your enthusiasm and wish you luck with such a task.'

But right now Edward was feeling decidedly poorly. When he had reached the outskirts of Chester, most of the opposition had melted away. A few bands of Welshmen had unsuccessfully tried to harass his advance to the town, but when Edward himself had led a chase to the marauders, an arrow had caught him in the thigh. His doctor had seen to the wound and applied a makeshift bandage. It seemed nothing at the time and added to one of three or four wounds the King had received in past conflicts and battles.

On his arrival at Chester, the reputation of the King had frightened the Mercian traitors and their ealderman, who had fled the town. The rest of the town immediately surrendered Chester to their King and he entered unopposed through the entrance of the fortifications that his sister had designed and ordered to be built. In the aftermath, Edward would order that these defences would be made even stronger.

But there had been no conflict with the local communities or anyone else, even the Viking population over the last week or two of the excursion into the northern territories. In fact, not only did the communities of Mercia accept Edward as their King and Lord but in many towns such as Shrewsbury, to where the Saxon army was heading back, the people had heard of the King's approach and had come out onto the street to welcome him and cheer his men.

Athelstan rode up close alongside his father. 'We should make Shrewsbury the day after tomorrow, Father.'

The King nodded and grunted. Athelstan looked concerned. He was suddenly aware that his father was not well. He was slumped further forward in his saddle than his usual upright stance and he looked pale and troubled. 'Are you feeling alright, Father?'

'Not so good. We must stop shortly.'

'Just up ahead there is the village of Farndon. Aunt Athelflaed built a Royal house there. A good place to rest for the night. I will send Cuthbert and the scouts on ahead and warn them.'

It started to rain, a steady drizzle. Twenty minutes later they arrived at Farndon, and the Elder of the Saxon community and many of the residents had come to welcome the King, but as Edward approached and started to dismount, he fell from his horse! There was a gasp from all around. He lay on the ground and seemed unable to rise to his feet. Athelstan ordered his men to carry the King to the Royal house that the village had prepared for him. He was laid on a bed.

They tried to give the King sustenance, but apart from a few sips of water, he refused any offering. Athelstan didn't like the look of this at all. He ordered Cuthbert, now wearing a badge which officially designated him as the King's chief scout, to Shrewsbury, where they had arranged to meet with the Queen, along with her children and Archbishop Athelm, who had succeeded Plegmund.

'Request for the Queen to come to Farndon immediately. Tell her the King's health is very poor.'

Athelstan was becoming alarmed and feared the worst. He had to take measures to prepare in case his father's condition grew worse. Luckily, now that Chester had been resolved, the situation in England, as his father had suggested, looked reasonably calm and settled.

The next day, Saturday, the King was no better. In fact, he seemed to have declined further and was eating very small amounts. He spoke little despite Athelstan's efforts to converse with him. He had been trying to find the best doctors and one had examined the King at midday.

On inspecting the leg, the makeshift bandaging was removed. It was dirty and very bloody. The wound was dirty and still weeping blood, but the purple colour of the leg was of great concern.

'So what is the diagnosis? Is it serious?'

'Yes, Sire. I believe the arrow has poisoned his blood. Either it had been laced with poison or the wound has become badly infected.'

'What can be done?'

The man shook his head and said nothing but looked down at the floor. Athelstan sighed.

On Sunday Cuthbert escorted the Queen into Farndon. In tow was her young four-year-old son Edmund with his baby sister Edburga and one-year-old baby brother Eadred, who had just learned to walk and was tottering around the courtyard, unaware of the events happening before him.

When they entered the King's room, Edward roused a little when he saw them.

'Why, Eadgifu, you didn't need to rush here with the children.' His voice was weak, but he managed a smile at the young Edmund, who was looking wide-eyed at his father, not used to seeing him in his bed in daytime. 'You have grown, Edmund. I am sure you will be a tall and handsome man when you are older, and who knows, one day you may be King!' Little did Edward realise that there were three future kings standing in the room before him.

The Queen ordered her maid to usher away the children. She could see that her husband was very ill and so she sat by his bed and held his hand. She looked up at Athelstan, who gave a weak smile, but he felt obliged to explain to her, when he had the chance, what the doctor had said the day before.

The Archbishop entered the room, briefly speaking to Athelstan, then sitting in the corner of the room and saying prayers for the King, who beckoned to Athelstan to come closer. He also gestured for his clerk to step forward with a document he had prepared earlier.

'I feel wretched, my son.' There was a pause. 'My clerk here carries a list of people who need to be rewarded for their service to me. Please make sure that this is carried out without delay.'

Athelstan took the list from the clerk and read out loud the names of those on the list, which contained a variety of men and women from different status and class. Not only family members but bishops, thegns, and ealderman.

'I will see to this, Father. You don't have to worry. Cuthbert is on this list and he is still here. Would you like to see him?'

'Yes, show him in.'

Cuthbert was soon found and hurried in to see the King, assuming it was another scouting task he would be requested to undertake. He was accompanied to the King's bed but was shocked to see him looking so pale and exhausted. His eyes were closed.

'Lord?'

Edward opened his eyes. 'Ah, Cuthbert, I just wanted to tell you that your contribution to my endeavours has been enormous and cannot be underestimated. I don't know what I would have done without you. You have been a loyal and true servant.' The King's breathing was shallow and rapid, and it suddenly dawned on Cuthbert that his King was dying. His eyes filled with tears.

'It has been a great honour and a privilege, My Lord.'

'You deserve to be rewarded.' He signalled to the bishop and his clerk. Cuthbert was expecting the usual silver coin, but the bishop presented him with a scroll.

'This scroll contains a grant of land in Essex not too far from your beloved hometown of Maldon. You will be a thegn of this manor.'

'I… I am so grateful, My Lord.'

'The least I can do.'

Cuthbert had very mixed emotions: elation that he should now be a landowner and that the King had thought so highly of him, but regret that the King's life seemed to be ebbing away and his own future was uncertain. But as he was leaving he found Athelstan alongside him.

'I hope you will scout for me in the future, Cuthbert?'

'Why, yes, most definitely, My Lord. Thank you.'

'I think it is I who should thank you for your past

services and assistance you have given to the King.'

Athelstan returned to Edward's bedside, where the King spoke in a weak voice. 'I hope I have acted in a way befitting for a King and that God will forgive me for my misdoings.'

'Yes, Father. You are revered by the English people. As for God... I am not qualified to assess your conduct but you appear to have been well-meaning and gracious.'

'I am glad you say English and not Saxon people. If I cannot go on, as it seems, you must continue my mission to bring together the people of this realm and unify the regions into one kingdom. I could not have achieved what I have without the help of my sister. It is important that our family stick together and support each other.' Edward paused, trying to remember what was important to tell his son. 'I have left a will naming you as my successor. The Vikings have been a thorn in my side and will no doubt be trouble for you too. If only they would accept Christianity.

'...I feel so tired. I... I... need to sleep...'

Edward closed his eyes. Athelstan left the room and made arrangements for the return journey to Winchester. But a few hours later the archbishop's servant appeared, looking frantic. 'My Lord, come quick... it's the King.'

Athelstan rushed back into the house. The archbishop was leaning over the King's body making the sign of the cross. Athelstan looked at Eadgifu, who had a tear rolling down her cheek. As the archbishop stood back he leant down and kissed his father on his forehead. The mournful young Queen looked up at him.

'He wished to be buried in his New Minster.'

'Yes.'

'You will look after us, won't you, Athelstan?'

'Of course. Have no fear. I will take care of my younger brothers and sisters. The King was right. Edmund may be king one day, for I have no desire to marry or have children of my own. My duty is to God, the Church and the English people.'

'What about Alfweard?'

'I do not wish to have any conflict with him. I hope we can work together. But I am older and Father wished that I should be King and rule this land.'

'I hope you will make a good king, Athelstan.'

Athelstan stepped out into the air and walked over to the ridge. He could see far into the distance, with the trees and the fields all around. It was mid-afternoon in July. The rain had cleared and it was stifling hot, but Athelstan did not notice the heat because he was deep in thought. He could see a farmer below him, haymaking in his field. He felt the weight of responsibility on his shoulders. His big hope was that this was going to be his kingdom and that his countrymen would support him as King. He looked to the sky as a hawk circled above him.

CHAPTER 14
THE FIND
A SECONDARY SCHOOL IN ESSEX'S HISTORY CLASS

'What happened after Edward's death then, Sir? Did Athelstan become King?'

'Ah, yes but it wasn't quite as straightforward as a simple succession. Athelstan was elected by the Mercian Witan as King. But in Wessex, where he had had little influence, the council offered the crown to Alfweard, who accepted. But just sixteen days later, he died and was buried at Winchester with his father.'

'Bit coincidental, isn't it? That he should die so soon after?'

'Foul play, you mean?' Mr Burchell smiled. 'Well, yes, I agree it was rather a coincidence. Athelstan is regarded as a noble king, but was it possible for him to engineer his half-brother's death? Well, maybe, but we have no way of knowing the true relationship between them. Or was it just a twist of fate? We shall never know. In any case Athelstan did indeed become King of all the Saxons, persuading Wessex by the following year to accept him. But more, he carried on where his father left off and conquered the kingdom of Northumbria. He is acknowledged as the first King of England, some say of Britain, because the King of Scotland and most of Wales also accepted him as their overlord. But he could only have achieved what he did because his father, not forgetting the assistance from his aunt, had laid the foundations of a united country.'

'Why was it called the Dark Ages then?'

'Good question. Not a phrase I like very much. Following the occupation by the Romans, who built roads, public baths, buildings with sewage and sanitation, and so on, it was considered that Britain took a more regressive step when the Saxons arrived. But more modern research has revealed that there was much more to the Saxon age than originally thought. It was when Christianity came to England, which arguably offered some sort moral code of behaviour. Trade was widespread, as artefacts that have been found in England are made of materials found in the far reaches of Europe and beyond.

'This is a very important period in our history because it is all about the making of England. Many communities, which did not exist during Roman times, sprang up all over the country, creating new towns, many fortified by Saxon burghs. Some, like Warwick, Birmingham and Bury St Edmunds, became important centres of commerce and administration. Here in Essex, places like Maldon became successful market towns. But most of all, dozens of smaller hamlets evolved in every county, which became the English village, as evidenced in the Domesday Book, nearly all ultimately with their own church and watermill. And in

Essex nearly all the villages and towns are of Saxon origin. Those places ending in -ing, -ham, -don and -ford all denote Saxon communities. Who can give me the examples of such places?'

'Maldon!'

'Witham.'

More hands went up.

'Chelmsford.'

'Margaretting and Ingatestone.'

'All correct. Also, the Anglo-Saxon language was the ancestor of the English language. Just as important, this was the time when the kingdoms of the old England began to fade as an entity after Edward. They still had provincial leaders, but for the most part, there was one overall king.

'But Edward seems to have been completely overshadowed by his father. True, most of the "grand plan" and the strategy of uniting Mercia and Wessex, building of the burhs and the standing army was undoubtedly Alfred's vision. But Edward actually achieved all this to a much greater extent than Alfred. If you look at the map of England in 899 and compare it with that in 924 when Edward died, there is a huge territorial difference. Yet I know of no known statue of Edward the Elder anywhere, although there is a statue of his sister at Tamworth. Anyway, the three generations of the family, from Alfred to his children and then his grandson Athelstan, produced some of the most outstanding leaders in England's history.'

'And after Athelstan?'

'So Athelstan never married and had no children. His young brother Edmund succeeded him at the age of eighteen and Edward's descendants continued to rule apart from a twenty-six-year period from 1016, when the Danish King Canute and his sons ruled. But the Saxons returned when Edward the Confessor succeeded and ruled until 1066. And we know what happened in that year.'

'So was 1066 the end of the Saxon royal house for good then?' enquired Leo.

'Well, not quite. It is worth mentioning two women who had an influence of the future genealogy. William the Conqueror's wife was Matilda, a direct descendant of Alfred the Great's younger daughter through generations of the Counts of Flanders. But more relevant, perhaps, is that Henry I, William's son, married Edith, a Saxon princess who became Queen of England, and she was a direct descendant of Edward the Elder. Their only surviving legitimate child when Henry died was Matilda, who married Geoffrey Plantagenet, and their son became Henry II, the ancestor of the future monarchs of England. Which is why, even today, our current Royal family can trace their roots directly back to Edward and Alfred and beyond.'

'The Saxon period was quite a lengthy dynasty then?'

'Absolutely! Over six hundred years of Saxon rule, one way or the other. By the eleventh century, England was already multi-cultural with a diverse background which now included Normans, Danish and Vikings. But the majority of the population was Anglo-Saxon, especially in the south and south-east. Even after 1066, despite Norman rule, it was still the case that England was culturally Anglo-Saxon in nature. What mystifies me is the awe that the Vikings seem to receive. They were good navigators and sailors, and some were voyagers looking to settle peacefully in Britain, but many were savage and confrontational, taking advantage of small, defenceless communities. And their reputation as fighting warriors was overrated in my opinion. In so many of the main battles between Saxons and Vikings, such as Edington, the Battle of the Holme, Tetenhall, Brunanburh, Stamford Bridge and so on, the Saxons were victorious.'

Just then the bell went for the end of the lesson and the pupils began to put their books away.

'Don't forget your homework. Draw a Saxon family tree for at least three generations and include Alfred, Edward, Athelflaed and Athelstan. See you all next Monday.'

BRADWELL

It was a beautiful warm and sunny Sunday morning in June. Leo's favourite subject at school was history, and following his lesson the week before, he had embarked on his own reading of the Saxon era. He had already read a book on Alfred the Great and he was now sitting in the lounge, reading another on the Saxon kings. He had just finished the chapters on Edward the Elder and Athelstan when his father entered the room.

Leo asked him if they could journey out to the old Saxon Chapel of St Peter on the Wall at Bradwell-on-Sea for a stroll.

'Good idea,' responded his dad. 'Just what's needed on a lovely day like this. We can take a packed lunch.'

They travelled to the Dengie Peninsular and through Bradwell village, parking at the end of the track, and walked along to the little Saxon church. This is a remote part of Essex, and the church stands alone in a field overlooking the North Sea. To the north is the estuary of the River

Blackwater and on the other side of the river can be seen Mersea Island.

Leo, with his love of history, found the little chapel fascinating. Built around the year 660 from brick and stone that came from the Othona Roman fort that once existed there, it is one of the oldest surviving Christian buildings in England. It was built on the instructions of St Cedd, who came to this part of Essex to spread Christianity to Sigberht, the King of the East Saxons. It would have been regarded as a cathedral in Saxon terms. In the Middle Ages it suffered a fire so had to be repaired and was used as a church again until it fell into disrepair and so it was used as a barn in the nineteenth century by a local farmer. In 1920 it was restored and re-consecrated as a chapel, later having Grade I listed status. Today it is regularly used as a church again and is open to the public, as the chapel door is never locked.

Leo went down to the beach. His dad enjoyed the peaceful surroundings and Leo threw stones into the water. They sat and ate their packed lunch of sausage rolls and egg sandwiches.

'Hey, Dad! Look at the that!' he said, pointing out to sea at a large sailing vessel with a big brown sail.

'Oh, that's one of the old Thames barges. They are over one hundred years old. They carried coal and other cargo up the River Thames to London. Although they are very large vessels they could be sailed by just two men. It looks like *Kitty* moored at Maldon, although usually she doesn't come up this far. These days most of the barges are privately owned and are used for sailing trips up and down the river.'

As the boat got nearer, Leo imagined it as a Viking longship sailing towards the coast of Essex, filled with invading Danish warriors.

Before going back, Leo took out his metal detector from the boot of the car and went hunting for treasure in the fields around. He spent a little while in the trees and then along by a ditch but without success. After a while his dad called out, 'Time to go, Leo. Your mother will have the dinner ready and will be wondering where we are.

'Okay.' And just as he took the last swing of his detector a bleep sounded. Leo brushed away the leaves and twigs around the long grass and got out his little trowel. Probably a bottle top or something equally unexciting. The object was only an inch or two below the surface. He grabbed it with his fingers and extracted what looked like a disc from the ground a little more than two inches in diameter. Hang on, this was no ordinary object.

'Dad, I've found something!' He wiped away as much of the dirt and grime that he could.

'What is it?' His dad gave Leo a handkerchief to 'polish up' the item. There was blue and gold in the metal and it was beautifully ornate. 'Looks like some sort of brooch, Leo.' As they cleaned it up it became evident that it was clearly an item of jewellery, but it was difficult to ascertain how old it was. If there had been a clasp on the back, it no longer existed.

'This could be very old, Leo. If it is genuine, well, it may be many hundreds of years old.'

Leo was smiling broadly. What a find! He couldn't wait to get home and show it to his mum. Where did it come from? And who had it belonged to? When was this lovely object lost in the long grass by the ditch? So many unanswered questions.

'Maybe I will take it to the curator of the museum in Southend and see if he can shed any light on its date.'

Leo thought that was a very good idea.

That day had been something to remember. Leo felt very excited and pleased with his find. He made his way back down the grassy track towards the car with his father.

But who was that following behind? The ghostly figures of Saxon thegns carrying their shields, with their swords glinting in the sunlight. And leading them, sitting proudly on a beautiful and majestic white horse, the son of Alfred the Great and King of the Saxons, Edward the Elder.

APPENDIX 1
THE SAXON FAMILY TREES

The Saxon Family Tree

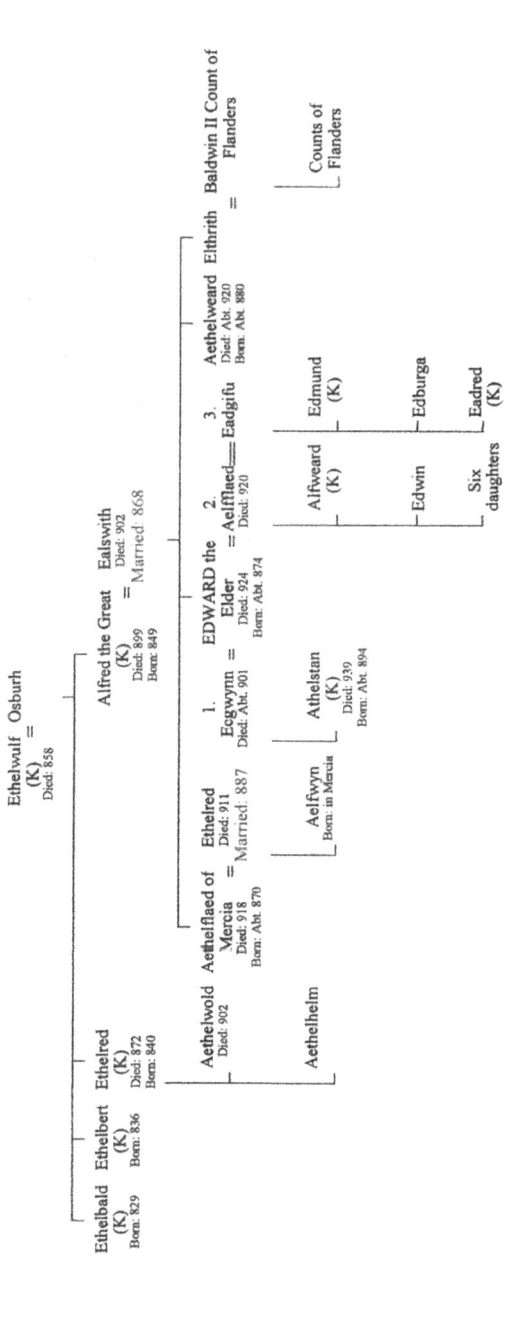

Ethelwulf = Osburh
(K)
Died: 858

Children of Ethelwulf:
- Ethelbald (K) Born: 829
- Ethelbert (K) Born: 836
- Ethelred (K) Died: 872, Born: 840
- Alfred the Great (K) Died: 899, Born: 849 = Ealswith Died: 902, Married: 868

Children of Alfred the Great and Ealswith:
- Aethelflaed of Mercia Died: 918, Born: Abt. 870 = Ethelred Died: 911, Married: 887
  - Aelfwyn Born: in Mercia
- EDWARD the Elder (K) Died: 924, Born: Abt. 874
  - 1. Ecgwynn Died: Abt. 901
    - Athelstan (K) Died: 939, Born: Abt. 894
  - 2. Aelflaed Died: 920
    - Alfweard (K)
    - Edwin
    - Six daughters
      - Edburga
  - 3. Eadgifu
    - Edmund (K)
    - Eadred (K)
- Aethelweard Died: Abt. 920, Born: Abt. 880
  - Aethelwold Died: 902
    - Aethelhelm
- Elfthrith = Baldwin II Count of Flanders
  - Counts of Flanders

APPENDIX 2
HISTORICAL AND FICTIONAL CHARACTERS

Historical Figures		
Aelflaed		Second wife of Edward the Elder.
Aelfweard	Died 924	Edward's second son and King of Wessex for just sixteen days.
Aelfred (the Great)	Died 899	Father to Edward.
Aelfwynn		Daughter of Ethelred and Aethelflaed.
Aethelflaed	Died 918	Ruler and Lady of Mercia. Daughter of Alfred the Great.
Aethelred	Died 911	Saxon Lord of Mercia and husband to Aethelflaed.

Aethelstan	Died 940	Eldest son of Edward. Raised by King of England.
Aethelwold		Nephew of Alfred the Great. Contender to be King of Wessex in opposition to Edward.
Asser	Died 909	Bishop of Sherborne. Biographer to Alfred.
Athelhun	Died 922	Bishop of Worcester who succeeded Werferth.
Athelm	Died 926	Archbishop of Canterbury who succeeded Plegmund.
Athelweard	Died abt 920	Younger brother to Edward. Had two sons, both killed at battle of Brunanburh in 937.
Charles III of West Frankia (France)	Died 929	Husband of Eadgifu and father to Louis IV of France.
Constantine II	Died 943	King of Scotland.
Cyfeiliog		Bishop of Powys and the Welsh borders.
Denewulf	Died 908	Bishop of Winchester.
Eadgifu of Kent	Died 968	Third wife of Edward. Mother to Kings Edmund and Eadred, whom she outlived. Died during the reign of her grandson, Edgar.
Eadgifu		Daughter of Edward. Married Charles the Simple.

Ealdred	Died 933	King or Ruler of Bernicia in Northumbria.
Ealswith	Died 1902	Mother to Edward and wife of Alfred.
Edward the Elder	Died 924	King of Wessex and the Saxons. Son of Alfred.
Egwina		First wife to Edward.
Eohric	Died 902	Last Viking king of Essex.
Eowils	Died 910	Viking king who invaded Northumbria.
Frithstan		Bishop of Winchester who succeeded Denewulf.
Grimbald (Saint)	Died 901	Abbott of the New Minster and advisor to the Kings of Wessex.
Haldane		Viking King who invaded Northumbria.
Harald		Viking Earl who invaded the West Country.
Ingrimund	Died 910	Irish Viking who settled in the Wirral.
Louis IV of West Frankia	Died 954	Son of Eadgifu and grandson of Edward.
Ohter		Viking earl who invaded the West Country.
Plegemund	Died 923	Archbishop of Canterbury.
Ragnall	Died 921	Viking ruler of Northumbria. Died at York.

Sigehelm	Died 902	Ealdorman of Kent and father of Eadgifu. Killed at the Battle of the Holme.
Sihtric	Died 927	King of York succeeding Ragnall.
Werferth	Died 915	Bishop of Worcester.

Saints		
St Cedd	Died 664	Founder of the Christian community at Bradwell in the seventh century.
St Cuthbert	Died 687	Northumbrian monk of the seventh century.
St Oswald	Died 642	Seventh-century king of Northumbria. His bones were taken from Viking territory in 909 and re-interred in St Oswald's Priory, Gloucester.
St Werbergh	Died 700	A shrine to St Werbergh was established at the Church of St Peter and St Paul at Chester. In 975, the Church of St Peter and St Paul was re-dedicated to St Werburgh.

Fictional Characters		
Agnar		Son of Golderon and Gerth.
Aldwine		Leader (reeve) of the Maldon community.

Cuthbert		Eldest son of Aldwine and Edward's scout.
Edgar		Youngest son of Aldwine.
Edith		Aldwine's wife.
Edmund		Saxon thegn loyal to Edward.
Edwin		Second son of Aldwine.
		Wife of Aldwine.
Galan		Brother of Golderon.
Gerth		Viking warrior.
Golderon		Wife of Wulfric, then Gerth then Edwin.
Guthrum		Danish invader of England, adversary to Alfred.
Harry		Twenty-first-century schoolboy.
Helvin		Athelflaed's informer at Chester.
Mildryth		Younger sister of Golderon and Galan.
Mr Burchell		Twenty-first-century history teacher.
Olaf		Leader of the Vikings invading Essex.
Wulfric		First husband to Golderon.

APPENDIX 3
THE SAXON BURGHS 910 TO 921

Towns known to be fortified by Edward (E) and Athelflaed (A) during Edward's reign. (From the *Anglo-Saxon Chronicles*.)

910	Bremesbyrig	A
912	Scergeat	A
	Bridgenorth	A
	Hertford	E
	Witham	E
913	Tamworth	A
	Stafford	A
	Eddisbury	A
	Warwick	A
914	Buckingham	E
915	Bedford	E
	Runcorn	A

916	Maldon	E
917	Towcester	E
	Wingingamere (Newport, Essex)	E
	Huntingdon	E
	Colchester	E
918	Derby	A
	Stamford	E
	Nottingham	E
919	Thelwall	E
	Manchester	E
920	Nottingham	E
	Bakewell	E
921	Cledemutha (Rhuddlan, North Wales)	E

APPENDIX 4
EDWARD'S CHILDREN

MARRIAGE 1, ECGWYNN

- Athelstan born about 894, King of England 924–939. *No issue.*
- N.B. there are some sources that mention he had a daughter, probably illegitimate, named Edith.

MARRIAGE 2, AELFFLAED OF WESSEX

- Aelfweard born about 901, King of Wessex for sixteen days in 924. *No issue.*
- Edwin born abt 905? Died 933. *No issue.*
- Aethelhild of Wilton Abbey. *No issue.*
- Eadgifu born abt 902? Married Charles the Simple, King of the West Franks. *They had one son: Louis IV of France.*

- Eadflaed born abt 903, of Wilton Abbey. *No issue.*
- Eadhild born abt 907? Married Hugh the Great, Duke of the Franks. *No issue.*
- Edith (Eadgyth) born abt 910, married Otto the Great, Holy Roman Emperor. *Two children: Luidolf, Duke of Swabia, and Liutgarde, Duchess of Lorraine.*
- Aefgifu married a prince of Burgundy?

MARRIAGE 3 EADGIFU OF KENT

- Edmund, King of England, born abt 920, reigned 939–946. *Sons Eadwig and Edgar both became kings of England (after Eadred).*
- Eadburh (St) born about 922, Nunnaminster, Winchester. *No issue.*
- Eadred born about 923, King of England 946–955. *No issue.*

APPENDIX 5
TIMELINE

868	Marriage of Alfred and Ealhswith.
870	Probable birth date of Athelflaed. Vikings murder St Edmund and sack Peterborough.
871	Alfred becomes king.
874	Probable birth date of Edward.
878	Battle of Edington. Vikings defeated.
887	Probable marriage date of Athelflaed and Ethelred.
890	Plegemund becomes Archbishop of Canterbury.
893	Marriage of Edward to Ecgwynn. Edward fights the Vikings at the Battle of Farnham.
894	Birth of Athelstan.
899	Death of King Alfred. Edward becomes king. Marriage of Edward and Alflead.
900	Athelwold claims the throne and takes Wimborne.

902	Battle of the Holme. Athelwold killed.
908	Death of Denewulf, Bishop of Winchester.
909	Asser dies.
910	Battle of Tettenhall. A decisive Saxon victory.
911	Ethelred dies. Athelflaed becomes Lady of the Mercians.
912	King Edward marches to Maldon.
914	Viking Earl Ohter seizes Bishop Cyfeiliog and his ransom is paid by Edward.
916	King Edward revisits Maldon and fortifies the town.
917	Colchester besieged and taken by the Saxons. Vikings besiege Maldon but are put to flight. East Anglia and Essex submit to Edward.
918	Athelflaed dies at Tamworth. Elfwyn enters Holy Orders.
919	Marriage of Edward and Eadgifu. Plegemund dies.
920	Submission of rulers to Edward at Bakewell.
924	Edward dies. Athelstan becomes king.
927	Athelstan receives the kingdom of Northumbria. At Eamont Bridge Athelstan becomes overlord in virtually all of Britain, recognised as the first King of England.

REFERENCES AND FURTHER READING

Anglo-Saxon Chronicles, Translated by Ann Savage, 1982, Phoebe Phillips, ISBN: 978-0-8628-8440-6

Edward the Elder and the Making of England, Harriet Harvey Wood, 2018, Sharpe Books, ISBN: 978-1-9808-7858-2

The Warrior Queen: The Life and Legend of Aethelflaed, Joanna Arman, 2017, Amberley Publishing, ISBN: 978-1-4456-8279-2

Alfred's Britain: War and Peace in the Viking Age, Max Adams, 2017, Zeus Ltd, ISBN: 978-1-7840-8031-0

The Saxon Kings, Richard Humble, 1980, George Weidenfeld and Nicolson Ltd & Book Club Associates, ISBN: 978-0-2977-7784-7

Anglo-Saxon England, Oxford History of England, Sir Frank Stenton, 1943, Oxford University Press, ISBN: 0-19-821716-1

There are very many websites, too numerous to list here. Below is a selection of useful ones:

https://www.realmofhistory.com/2016/09/17/10-facts-anglo-saxons-warriors/
https://www.totallytimelines.com/edward-the-elder-874-924/
https://www.historic-uk.com/HistoryMagazine/DestinationsUK/AngloSaxonSites/
https://www.thoughtco.com/women-of-the-tenth-century

VENUES

West Stow, Anglo-Saxon Village and Country Park, IP28 6HG
www.weststow.org
Tel: 01284 728718
Archaeological site, reconstructed village and museum with visitor centre and cafe.

Sutton Hoo, Saxon Royal burial and archaeological site, IP12 3DJ
www.nationaltrust.org.uk/sutton-hoo
Tel: 01394 389700

ABOUT THE AUTHOR

LAURIE PAGE is a fully qualified history teacher that has a particular interest in England in the Middle Ages, who has previously authored *Essex Walks into History*. Apart from being an avid reader of history, Laurie spends time researching genealogy, which he taught at Adult Education Centres for over 20 years. Born in Essex, he now lives in Martock, Somerset. He has one son who lives in Winchester, which is strongly featured in the novel.

NAME AND PLACE INDEX

Aelfflaed 15-18, 36, 137
Aethelfrith 36
Agnar 81-82, 152
Aldwine (Ealderman) 19-23, 47-54, 77-78, 83-84, 108-109, 115-119, 151-152
Alfred (King) 3-9, 13, 16, 21, 22, 25-26, 60-63, 126, 164-166, 168
Alfweard 26, 85, 119-120, 123, 127, 142, 153, 161, 162
Archenfield 87
Asser 5-7, 13, 15, 55, 63, 65
Athelflaed (Lady of Mercia) 3-4, 9-10, 25-29, 36, 39-45, 58, 61, 67 69-73, 85-86, 90, 92, 94-95, 99, 123, 104-105, 125-126, 128-132, 143, 153, 156, 164, 166
Athelhelm 15
Athelhun (Bishop) 128-133
Athelm (Archbishop) 157-158, 160
Athelney (Somerset) 61
Athelstan 1-2, 9, 13, 18, 26, 28-29, 39-43, 45, 58-63, 69-71, 85, 94-100, 123, 125, 128-132, 134, 137, 142, 153-154, 156-161, 162, 164, 166
Athelweard (Edward's brother) 3, 11-12, 30, 36-38, 66, 79-80, 126-127, 133-134, 142, 154
Athelwold 7-10, 12-13, 21-24, 27, 28-29, 31-34, 37, 137
Augustine (Saint) 145

Bakewell 141
Bamburgh 126, 144, 155
Bedford 105-106, 122
Benfleet 60
Bernicia 126, 147
Birmingham 163
Blackwater(River) 20, 48, 54, 79, 109, 151, 167
Blaise (Saint) 65
Bradbury Rings 10
Bradwell (Essex) 47-50, 54, 74, 78-79, 166-169
Bremesbyrig 67
Brunanburgh (battle) 166
Brycheniog 126
Buckingham(shire) 36, 86, 104, 109-110
Burchell (Mr) 1. 161-166
Burhs 36
Bury St Edmunds 163

Cambridge 106
Canterbury 134-135
Cedd (Saint) 167
Ceolmund (bishop) 83
Charles (King) 135, 138-140, 154
Chelmer (River) 54
Chelmsford 164
Chester 39-45, 72, 155, 157
Chippenham 15, 61, 87-90, 92, 98
Christchurch 9, 11-12
Cnute 165
Colchester 111-114, 119, 122
Colosseum 64
Constantine 125-126, 144, 146-147, 155
Cooling (Kent) 136
Corbridge 144
Cornwall 55
Crediton 55
Cuthbert (Maldon) 19, 22, 24, 28-29, 30-32, 35-38, 67-70, 76-78, 83-84, 86-92, 94-95, 99-105, 111-112, 114-115, 120, 122-123, 131 133, 135, 152, 156-159
Cuthbert (Saint) 63, 85
Cyfeiliog (Bishop) 86-87, 91-93, 104

Danelaw 22, 36, 67, 100, 126, 132, 141
Dee (river) 40-42
Deira 126
Denewolf (bishop) 7-8, 15-18, 55
Dengie (Essex) 74, 152, 166
Derby 125, 129, 141
Devon 55
Domesday 163
Dover 135
Dublin 39

Eadgifu (Edward's daughter) 134-136, 138-140, 154
Eadgifu (Queen) 136-137, 157-158, 160
Eadred 157
Eadhild 134-136
Ealdred 126, 144, 146-147, 155
Ealswith, (mother of Edward) 3

East Anglia 21, 29-30, 49, 62, 125, 133, 143
Ecgwynn, (first wife of Edward) 3, 9, 12
Edburga 157
Edgar (Maldon) 20, 48, 53, 73-76, 79-81, 83-84,
115-116, 149-150, 152
Edington (Battle of) 61, 166
Edith (Maldon) 20, 49, 53, 77-78, 83, 117, 151-152
Edith (Queen) 165
Edmund (thegn) 11, 72, 93, 101-104, 135
Edmund (Saint) 111
Edmund (son of Edward) 157-158, 161, 164
Edward I 1
Edward the Confessor 1, 165
Edward the Elder 1-13, 15-17, 23, 24-29, 30-31, 35-36, 40, 55-65, 66, 68, 71-73, 77-80, 82, 85-92, 97, 99-103, 105-110, 111-114, 119-120, 122-123, 125, 127-128, 131-140, 141-147, 152, 153-160, 162, 164-166, 168
Edward the Martyr 1
Edwin (Maldon) 19-21, 23-24, 30-31, 35-38, 47-50, 52-54, 67-69, 71, 73-77, 79-84, 86-93, 99, 110, 115-116, 118-120, 149-152
Edwin (son of Edward) 85
Egberht 126

Egbert (king) 7
Egbert's Stone 61
Elfwyn 26-28, 59, 128, 130-134
Elswitha 25
Eohric (King of Essex) 22-23, 28, 33-34, 37
Eowils 66, 73
Essex 20, 22, 28-29, 60, 78, 125, 133, 143,
159, 163, 166-168
Ethelred (king) 6, 8
Ethelred (of Mercia) 9-10, 25-29, 30, 32, 36, 39-40, 58-59,

Ethelred 63, 69, 73

Farndon 153, 156-157
Farnham (Battle of) 59
Flanders 165
Franks (Francia) 107, 109, 135, 139, 154
Frisia (kingdom of) 20, 56, 83, 107
Frithestan (Bishop) 142, 147

Galan 47, 84, 114-115, 120-122, 149-151
Goeffrey Plantagenet 165
Gerth 52, 74, 81
Gloucester 25, 27, 39, 45, 58, 68, 90, 92, 94-95,
97, 99-100, 123, 132-134
Goda 136
Golderon 19-20, 47, 49, 51-52, 54, 74-75, 80-82, 84, 114, 117,

120, 152
Grimbald 24
Guthrum (Danish King) 21, 61-62, 125

Haldane 66, 68-69, 73

Harald (Dane) 86, 89-90, 97-99
Harold II (King) 1
Helvin 39-40
Henry I 165
Hereford 97
Hertford 3
Holme (battle of) 34-35, 137, 166
Hugh (Duke of Franks) 135

Imar 145
Ingatestone (Essex) 164
Ingimund 39, 42, 44-45, 72
Ireland (Irish) 39, 40, 44, 46, 121, 144-145
Itchen (river) 56, 58

Kent 29, 32-33, 37-38, 59, 83, 136-137
Kingsholme 94
Kings Worthy 56, 58
Kingston upon Thames 7
Kitty (boat) 167

Leicester 125, 129, 131
Leo(schoolboy) 1-2, 162-169
Leo V (Pope) 64
Lincoln 125, 132
Lindisfarne

Litchfield 68
London 60, 167
Lotharingia 139

Maldon 19-22, 28, 31, 47, 49, 52, 73, 76-79, 81, 107, 110, 114-117, 122, 142, 149-152, 159, 163-164, 167
Malmesbury 15
Margaretting (Essex) 164
Marozia 64
Mary (abbey of Saint) 133
Matilda (wife of William I) 165
Matilda (daughter of Henry I) 165
Mercia 3, 7, 9-10, 25-27, 29, 40, 42, 63, 66, 69-70, 73, 86-87, 104-105, 121-122, 125, 12-134, 143, 153-155, 162, 164
Mersea Island (Essex) 167
Mersey (River) 40, 86, 94
Mildryth 47-48, 74-75, 81-84, 114, 117, 120, 123, 149-150
Minehead 100

New Minster 5, 25, 58, 160
Northampton 105

Normandy 138-139
Northumbria 7, 66, 68, 70, 73, 96, 121, 126, 128, 147, 154-155, 132, 143-144, 146-147, 163
Norwegians 39-40, 43, 145
Nottingham 125, 133, 141
Nunnaminster 25, 65, 133

Ohter (Dane) 86, 89, 92-93, 95, 97, 99-100, 104
Olaf 51-52
Oswald's Priory (St) 94, 132-133
Othona (Roman fort) 167
Ouse (River) 86, 104, 106
Owain 125, 146
Oxford 29

Penk (River) 67
Peter (Saint) 64, 166
Peterborough 30, 35
Pewet Island 50
Plegmund (Archbishop) 3, 5-6, 13, 25, 28, 35-36, 55-56, 63, 66, 68, 134-135, 157
Porlock 101

Ragnall 126, 129, 142-146, 154
Ramsey 55
Reims 135
Richard III 1
Rochester 59, 83
Rollo 138-139
Rome / Romans 42, 45, 54-56, 58, 63-, 111, 163
Ronan 43-45

Saint Lawrence Bay 74
Salisbury 15, 18
San Lorenzo 64
Sandwich 56
Scandinavia 145-146
Scotland 57, 125-126, 141, 143-144, 146-147, 163

Sergius (Pope) 64
Severn (River) 67, 86, 88, 97-98, 102-103
Sherbourne 63
Shoebury (Essex) 60
Shrewsbury 156
Sigehelm 29, 31-34, 37, 137
Sihtric 144, 154-155
Somerset 55, 61, 100
Stamford 125, 129, 131-132
Stamford Bridge (battle) 166
Steepholm (island) 103
Strathclyde 125, 142, 146

Tadcaster 129
Tamworth 128, 131, 164
Tettenhall (battle of) 67, 88, 166
Tewdyr 126
Thames (River) 99, 167
Theodora 64
Theophylact 64
Thurcytel (Earl) 105-106, 109-110
Tiddingford 49
Tillingham (Essex) 49
Totham 48,
Trent (River) 141
Tudors 1

Uhtred 33-34
Wales (Welsh) 40, 57, 86-87, 95, 104, 126, 142-143, 146, 155, 163
Warwick 94, 163
Watchet 99-101
Wells 55

Werburgh (St) 45
Werferth (Bishop) 41-43, 45
Wessex 5-7, 9-10, 23, 26, 36, 55, 61-63, 71, 78, 99, 127, 134, 142-143, 154, 162, 164
William I 165
Wiltshire 55, 61
Wimborne 8-11
Winchester 3-8, 11, 17, 24, 27, 31, 35-38, 55-58, 80, 84-85, 102, 104, 109-110, 123, 125-127, 132-134, 137, 142, 153, 160
Winchester (Bishop of) 85
Wirral 39, 42, 44
Witan (Council) 4-7, 127, 132-133, 162
Witham 48, 78-79, 164
Wolverhampton 67, 69
Worcester 28, 41, 109
Wulfric 19, 23, 49-50, 52

York 121, 126, 128, 141-144, 146, 154